MW01253258

Dream Untold
SEASON-1

BALAJI SIVARAJAN

INDIA • SINGAPORE • MALAYSIA

Notion Press

No.8, 3rd Cross Street
CIT Colony, Mylapore
Chennai, Tamil Nadu – 600004

First Published by Notion Press 2021
Copyright © Balaji Sivarajan 2021
All Rights Reserved.

ISBN 978-1-63781-481-9

Dedication

To the love of my life – Jayaprabha.

You inculcated the idea of writing my story into a book. You did not just stop there; you are my first reader of every draft, you are considerate when I act crazy, forgiving when I was busy day and night writing, friendly, encouraging and you took infinite places to stand by my side. I would have given this up a long time ago if it is not for your support.

Thank you, my dear wife.

Contents

Acknowledgements

Dream Untold is my dream come true. I would like to thank all who made this story turn a book.

First, my beloved Story-notebook and pen. You are the only guys who have seen me writing all my crazy ideas, thoughts, and original words.

Second, all the movies, novels, music and my eternal dreams that inspired me to envision this story.

Third, Google search, my dearest digital friend. You have all the references that I need at the right time.

Then...

Shahzia – friend in colleague, you travelled with me all this time, read all the chapters and shared your genuine comments. Thank you for encouraging me to keep writing this story.

Jaiganesh, you surprised me by reading the whole story overnight. Thank you for your review.

Nagaraj, thank you for your support and encouragement.

Mohith, my wonderful son and Deeyali, my lovely daughter.

My family, Akka and Mama, Kavitha and Yuvaraj, and Bavya kutty. My parents, Sivarajan and Lakshmi. My in-laws, Jayaraman and Rajeswari.

All my friends in India, UK, and USA. And, to all who believed in my story and encouraged me to write this book.

Notion Press:

Thank you, Akash, Shiny, Mridula and Martin who worked with me in the initial phase of the publishing process.

My consulting manager, Bhavika Kapoor, you heard all my ideas and feedbacks and guided me through all the process from cover design, copy editing and publishing the book with greatest patience. Thank you so much for being so supportive.

Special thanks to John Jasso – Design Team, copy-editing team and to all Notion Press friends who supported in the publishing process of this Book.

Finally, thank you, dear reader, for choosing *Dream Untold*.

Prologue

'Are you sure? Is it a good idea?' she asks.

'This is the right thing to do. I cannot carry this around anymore,' I answer along, packing my writing materials into my backpack.

'God...I don't know how to stop you...' she says.

'Please...not again...' I say.

'What if it changes everything, *da*? All you earned till date...'

Without responding, I complete packing.

Go near, I hold her face cheeks and kiss her naked lips.

'That is fine, you are here for me,' I say.

We smile.

'It may take me a long time to return. Take care. Wish me all the best,' I ask.

She hugs me tight.

Bid goodbye, I take leave.

New Chapter

'Thank you so much, Sanjay; you have been such a wonderful inspiration throughout my career,' I broke the sustained silence in the room.

'Thanks? Forget it. You still have a chance to withdraw your resignation,' he took his eyes off the monitor screen and rested them on me, fuming.

'I want to live my dream; and this is not the right place for it,' I started.

'Well, this is not the right time either,' he cut me and continued with his heated words. 'You have just started your career, Guru; quitting a job at this stage is ridiculous.'

For a second, those words startled me. Generally, corporate managers wouldn't voice out such concerns. Sanjay, however, was neither like the other rule-imposing managers nor was an awful boss. He took care of all his subordinates; and more than anyone, he cared a lot for me.

Nothing I could speak further; nor could my eyes face him. The very moment when I had first met him in that same conference room for the job interview, played on my mind. That was my first project, and the start point for everything that followed; I became Sanjay's favorite.

Project discussions, team meetings, preparations, escalations, appreciations, sleepless demanding work, and so many different shades of work I experienced in that very room! It went on to become the place for my resignation meeting too. My team was as close to my heart as Sanjay.

A beautiful resonance of memories flashed through my mind within a fraction of a second.

'I am gonna miss having an ideal boss and a wonderful team. And this resignation is gonna throw me into a world of anxiety,' I said to myself.

My conscience cautioned me, 'Don't go back on your decision now, stupid! After year-long discussions, advices from all corners, and complaining and crying, you have taken this decision. You have to stand by it.'

During my childhood, I'd befriended my conscience and had named him Tom, after Tom and Jerry. Like Tom, he'd used to chase this Jerry-Me, not to pounce on a prey, but as a bosom buddy to advice and act as a strict guard.

'Yes, I should stand by it,' I came back from my reverie.

'Okay! All the very best for your career or dream or whatever. If you need any help at any time, reach out to me, don't hesitate. And, if you are tired running behind your dream and decide to return, the doors are always open for you,' Sanjay interrupted with a manager's typical talk.

Clearing my throat, I bid goodbye to him and to my office.

Got to my feet, I returned near the door only to find it stuck. 'See, the door is not allowing me out,' I cried inside. 'The door is under maintenance, open the side door, you idiot,' Tom said sarcastically.

Laughing on the double thoughts, I marched towards the new chapter of my life.

'No more early morning wake ups, no office hurry ups, no day-to-night works and no hard feelings that it's not my dream,' I proclaimed.

A fresh life and a fresh start I had ahead of me where I could do everything I want. Everything, amidst the boredom of my home and listening to my parent's complain. In every middle-class Indian family, it's a crime failing to study engineering or not working for a renowned company. Their only son had quit his job to write and publish his own book; this wouldn't make all parents, to the least my parents happy.

Yes, my dream, all-time dream, was to write and publish a book. I gathered round a storyline, spending many late nights and weekends. A whale of time I'd got to develop, write and publish it.

Brain Child

'Almost a year I spent working on this story; a lot of research I conceived to fine-shape it,' I said in a firm tone.

'Good. This story is interesting. But there are challenges in publishing this book,' he paused. He picked the glass lid up to drink water. My heart propelled like a Ferrari engine at that pause.

'Challenges?' I asked.

'Yes, sir. It is in the science-fiction genre,' he said.

With utmost effort, I was fighting to convince the representative, Akhil Sankar, of KUBA Publications – a renowned publisher, to get my book published. Ironed white shirt tucked in grey color trousers, he perfectly resembled like one.

'But...' I started. Akhil cut in, 'Excuse me, I should attend this call, my boss...' he placed an hourglass on the table, picked the call in his cellphone and left the room.

My dry eyes rested on the liquid hourglass; I lost myself in my thoughts that rolled down along the liquid that dropped from the top into the bottom hourglass.

Science Fiction – 'Sci-Fi' genre stories had always fascinated me; eventually it was the genre I ended up writing my first book in. Scientific facts and technologies were a bundle of pursuit, binding them together by a true-to-life logic was one big task. Binding logic along with developing the actual story had bit a huge pie on my time. It took almost a year to complete the novel.

Techy explorations and scientific notions had forced me to travel to many places. Every second and every inch of travel had given a new lease of life to the story. The result was a fascinating, a scientific and colourful-perceptive fiction novel; I tried to perfect it after writing, re-writing and re-re-writing each and every page, choosing precise words.

Life hadn't been as favourable after resignation as I believed it would be. I neither had ample time to leisure nor peaceful mind to concentrate only on writing. Those office-go-work-and-go-home-sleep days were peaceful compared to the rough days I spent on the learning and the research to complete my debut Novel. Despite the pain, all those exploration-days never disappointed me.

"One should get impressed by his own art before anyone does" – that beautiful quote was my greatest driving energy. Writing is an art; each word I wrote had earnestly impressed me; more than just impression, a personal connect was established between us. The story was like a child to me, my own 'Brain-child,' which I'd given birth to.

All the pain a father and mother go through to give a childbirth, I went through. I had suffered both the painful dreams of a due mother and anxiety of a gracious father to complete that story. Yes, my own child.

'To be frank, I like your work, Mr?' Akhil entered the room and interrupted before I'd cry with my thoughts.

'Gunan Rudhra. Guru should do,'

'Yes, Mr Guru, after I read the script, I liked the clever story line and the neat narration,' he complimented.

'Thank you so much,' I acknowledged with a smile.

All those days, my cells were craving to sense some form of compliment. Conceiving this child was easier when it comes to delivering it. I'd mailed the manuscript to a dozen publishers. Mostly they were unanswered or returned. Kuba, however, was the first publication that called me in person.

'But the only concern is Sci-Fi genre,' he stood up and walked across the room.

'Is it a problem?'

'It is a different game for famous authors. For debutant, it is hard to market.'

'Really?' I jumped out of my skin.

'Yes, we don't have many Sci-Fi readers, you see.'

'This is my dream. I sacrificed my career for it and more than a dream, this is my life now,' my words troubled.

'I toootally understand.'

His accent irritated me.

'Can I suggest you something? Why don't you try writing a romance, a happening love story?'

'New story?' I started, Akhil interrupted. 'We love your work and narration, so I suggest you write a love story; I can assure publication. After that, immediately we will sit together to discuss this story,' he took his seat in front of me.

'I need time to rethink over this story. I have invested a year only on developing this story. After that, I have been busy for months searching and contacting publishers to proceed with publishing. Never I had time to work on any other story line. A romance story, that said, it's gonna be a complete new start,' I paused. Frustration pulled my voice down. I humbled, 'Can you please reconsider this story for further discussion? One last try?'

'Ok, but I am not sure about it.'

Anyone could clearly read his tone, 'No buddy, try some other story or some other publisher,' it sounded.

'Thank you,' I walked out lost in hope.

Nevertheless, that conversation did cheer all my hunger cells; the first official appreciation for my work gave a new hope.

Tom, my conscience, said, 'Perhaps, what he says makes sense. Very few science fiction movies are being made in India, it obviously echoes for novels as well. So why can't you give a new try?'

'That's true. I'm a debutant author and the only publicity for my work is word-of-mouth from people. If it's a romance story, the possibility of attracting the readers will be high, won't it?' I replied within.

'Hold on, so you are convinced for a fresh start?' Tom asked curiously.

Stepping inside the car, I buckled up. Twisting the key, the engine started.

'Ethaiyumae Thangidum

Idhayam Endrum Marathu...

Ethaiyumae Thangidum

Idhayam Endrum Marathu...

Nalai Namadhae, Nalai Namadhae

Nalai Namadhae, Nalai Namadhae...'

M.G.R's philosophical lines on the FM Put a smile on my face. I said, 'Fuck it...all I got is to try.'

Faithfully, I did so. Found a few more promising publishing houses who were worth contacting, I bettered my synopsis, added a couple of more plot-revealing chapters, and couriered them.

Days rolled down into the weeks. Never did I stop pushing myself to knock on any possible door. Doors were not just locked but sealed.

Baby or Love

'Akhil sent his third and final reminder note, on behalf of KUBA Publications, to consider their offer. I think it's time to move on,' I said.

'Really?' Mannu raised her eyebrows.

Mandhakini, I love calling her Mannu, was my cool and confident best friend since my school days. We completed engineering from the same university. The IT world had enticed me; college placement had paved the path to succeed in that want and employed me in a well-known software consulting multinational. On the other hand, Mannu had desired to become a stock market consultant and had prepared for a Post Graduate Program in Management. Stubborn and always well-devised what to do, she'd stuck to that decision.

Mannu was amazing in the way she dressed, conversed and carried herself, and I, a typical-next-door-guy, was neither the dashing nor the appalling kind. She helped a lot to enhance my appearance to fit into the corporate world.

Routine software work wiped out my 'IT' fantasy and unveiled the fact that I was not fit for it. Many people were around who had really enjoyed and evolved out of what they were doing in the same industry. However, Software and I were not made-for-each-other. Parallelly, the passion for writing had started to take control over me. Ultimately, it led me on the path to resignation and get involved fully in writing.

Everything had gone well for Mannu. She'd gotten admitted into Bengaluru IIM, completed her masters, and had set her own financial consulting firm. She mostly worked from home; a stroke of luck it was for me. Most of my days on developing and completing the story were spent in her home.

Mannu was indeed more excited when the writing bug bit me. She was in fact the one who'd stood for me to convince my parents when I'd decided to quit and write. She didn't just stop there; she was my sole source of encouragement throughout my year-long writing journey.

After finishing each chapter of the story, I'd share it with her. She read them throroughy and fed me back with her genuine comments. Mannu was my proofreader, editor and reviewer. Like me, she also waited for that day my story would get published and my dream would come true.

'How long? How long should we wait? Apart from KUBA publications, we didn't get a response from one other publication,' I was worried.

'First, calm down. I am about to talk to you about that. Instead of traditional publishing, you can try self-publishing,' Mannu said.

'What is that?' I asked.

'Last week, an article was published on how self-publishing houses are changing the way books are produced. Using one of them, you can self-publish your book. You would get "high royalty",' she double-quoted last words on the air and continued. 'Royalty stuffs are not important but think about self-publishing.'

'Interesting, tell me more about it,' I curiously asked.

'Yes, it is. A dedicated team will guide you from cover design to publishing and marketing your book. After reading the article, I contacted one of the ventures and discussed your book in detail. I'm pretty much confident that publishing a book is no big deal.'

'It is quite relieving to hear. The butterflies in my stomach are gaining their wings back,' I laughed in relief.

'But the fact that Akhil told, still stands true.'

'Not again?' I put a confused face.

'You worked really hard for this story. Like many thousands of books, yours should not be left sleeping on the bookstores. A sturdy fan base should be built before this book gets published.'

'Can a hapless stranger in this shabby denim and t-shirt, awaiting his debut book release, build a fan base?'

'Stop that,' she giggled and continued. 'Consider this, you first publish a love story, which anyone can read, relate to and feel. It becomes a huge hit. Then obvious it is that you will get a fan following who will eagerly expect your next. Then you publish your sci-fi story. How's that?' she fussed raising her hands dramatically.

'Hold on! Isn't it what Akhil said?'

'No, the intention differs. He agreed that your story and narration is amazing, but he was afraid it may fail to hit the top charts in the market. What I say, use the same talent of story writing and narration to write a love story, publish it with KUBA or any other publisher or you can even self-publish, and we will use all marketing stats to smash the charts,' she jumped off the chair, shouting the last line.

Hearing her loud voice, Keerthi came in and asked, 'Hey, what happened?'

'Am I loud? Nothing, we were just chatting,' Mannu calmed her down.

'Coffee? I am gonna make one for me,' Keerthi asked. We both nodded a 'yes.'

Keerthi was Mannu's roomie; they shared an apartment.

After few minutes, coffee in hands, Mannu and I came to the balcony; my much-loved space in her home. A beautiful small sit-out with a hanging swing at its center.

'What if it fails?' I doubted.

'What?'

'What if the love story doesn't smash the chart?'

'Don't be all negative, *da*. God will be with you, trust me, give it a try.'

'God...huh...' I sighed.

'Don't make fun of God.'

'I am not in that mood to fight against your beliefs now.'

'God or Mother Nature it is, but a superior driving force is there beyond us. Trust in it. You must give the new story a good amount of time; clear your head to conceive a fresh story line. Simple, an intense and emotional love story this time.'

'Yeah, I understand. Love, intense love,' I chuckled.

'You are a vegetable. Don't you worry. Wherever you fail to pass on the feel, I'll pitch in.'

Yes, I was. Since my college days, even in office, I had no love breeze sweep off my feet. Any specific reason I could recollect? No. Many of our friends had even gossiped about me and Mannu but we never had the thought ourselves.

'Okay cool, it's time to decide what you are gonna do next. Publish this story or start a new one,' Mannu said.

'You are right, Mannu; I can't let this grow any further. Already enough months have been spent working on publishing the story. Let's decide today: baby or love. What is your thought?'

'Ok come, let's decide it,' she ran into her room. I followed her.

We were in her room. She put on her specs and stood in front of the white pull-down-board with a red marker in hand.

'No red. Let's go auspicious,' she threw the red and picked a green marker.

Like a KG kid, I sat before the board; my hands supporting my chin and laughing at her, expecting a kinder class from a teacher.

She wrote down three options:

1. Deliver your baby.

2. Fall for a love (story, I mean).

3. Ride two horses at once.

'Hey what's this new 3rd choice?' I shouted.

'No, it's not,' she struck through 3rd option and said, 'that won't be possible, you need a lot of time to publish and market the book. More time to work on the new story. You can't do both.'

'Hmmm, you are correct,' I agreed.

'Now two options are left,' hitting the board with marker, she did resemble a teacher.

'Which option will you opt for?'

'Doesn't the second one seem better?' she bounced the ball back at me.

'Hey, this story is like my first child. Should I ignore it? Reasons may be anything,' my words fell.

'Ignoring for a while to make it more grandeur and successful. Perhaps, it's time to fall for your first love,' she smiled.

'So?'

'Let's close today's class,' she underlined the option.

'A new love story,' we both announced in unison.

Desperate Search

Zip zeep – cars and heavy trucks passed in rush. On the highway, I stopped by the pizza pit for a quick bite. Hopped into my car, I resumed my road trip.

Decisions are always easy; the tough part is to cope with it. Spent over a month on developing a new story, I failed of success and decided to travel a long way out; not for any science research but in search of love – intense love, for the new story.

Packed cloths, writing essentials, and other musts in a duffle bag, I departed to Javadhu Hills – splendid green valleys and lofty scenic beauty, it's a place of paradise. During college days, our group of friends had visited that place.

My first story stayed put in mind and heart and I couldn't win moving away and start a fresh story yet. I was desperately in need of a change. I settled on climbing hills and blowing the cobwebs away. Along NH-4 highway road, I drove all alone. During all my previous drives, the only point of concentration would be my first story; it won't go off that easy. I believed a long road trip, sheer hills and a breath of fresh air would help clear my head.

Increasing the music volume, leaving the entire world behind, I sang along.

"Rakkama kaiya thattu

Puthu raagathil mettukkattu

Adi raakkoazhi mellangottu

Jaga jaga jaga jaa

Indha raasaavin nenjathottu

Jaga jaga jaga jaga jaga..."

Highway lone drive, ear-warming music and cheesy pizza bite, wow, it was one delicious ride.

Hours by-passed.

My phone rang and the name 'Abhi' flashed on it. I picked the call up, '*Machan*, where are you?'

'Highway drive done, *da*, climbing hills,' I replied.

'Super, *da*, you should reach soon. See you here,' he said and hung up.

Lowered the window glass, I let the wind in and inhaled the greenish-fresh air. Driving up the hill amongst wintry weather was a feast for the eyes.

'Splendid days are waiting, surrounded by nothing but virgin green,' I cried.

Tom countered, 'Dude, you ride to write, remember?'

'Yeah, yeah, I remember you, officer,' I laughed.

A glitzy apple-red sunset coloured the evening sky when I reached the resort. It was incredibly placed amidst lush greenery hills top. I parked my car and got down.

Abhi waved at me. We ran into each with open hands for a long-time-no-see-hug.

Abhi's uncle owned the guest resort. During college when our group of friends visited this hill, we had stayed here. The moment I thought of hills, Javadhu hills struck my mind. I had informed Abhi about my arrival beforehand and he had promised to take care of my bed and bread for the trip.

He took me upstairs to the room that he had arranged for my stay. I flung the bag over a corner and jumped on the bed. My body temperature started reacting to the chill climate. I rubbed my hands to feel warmth.

'Tea?' both asked in unison. We laughed at each other.

'Come,' he walked me to the roof via the side stairs.

'What the fuck?' I screamed at him; no fine word I could find, so I filled with globalized expression to exclaim at the ambiance.

A round fire pit table and couple of chairs were put in middle of the rooftop. There was a standing light at one corner and a speaker placed on the diagonal corner, belting out hand-picked passé songs.

We took our seats opposite to each other. A maid poured tea in our cups.

'Thanks, *ka. Neenga keela ponga*. Late *agum*,' Abhi said. She did so.

'It has been 5 years since we visited here, you remember?' he asked.

'Remember? I cherish those days. Ten of us made the best buddy gang... Hmm, now all spread across. Each running their own work-life-marathon,' I said. We laughed.

A long memory-sharing chat kickstarted at the roof top. Hot chai and retro music provided old buddies with a perfect time. We shared our life happenings, talked about our friends and were surprised at the twists and turns of life. I gave up my profession to choose writing, and so did Abhi. He chose a different kind – journalism.

After a while, some music-sound came from downstairs; we went to the corner and checked out. On an open space next to the resort, a group of friends were singing loudly and danced around the campfire. Our college memories caught hold of us; we too had campfired right in that same place and had tribal danced around.

'Golden days,' I smiled.

Time flew away as we talked. Somewhere in between the chat, we had our dinner. Early in the morning we ended our long-happy-talk when he was about to leave.

'Are you sure you must leave?' I asked.

'*Ama, da.* Some business shot's press conference. CM, central ministers, and many big shots are gathering. I cannot miss it,' he said.

'I thought you will hang around for a couple of days,' I was upset.

'Last minute call from office, sorry, *da*. In fact, I stayed back to catch up with you.'

'Good that you did. I needed it,' we hugged.

'All the best for you story. I am waiting for that day when I will hold your novel in my hand,' he smiled.

No words to thank, I acknowledged with a smile.

He left. I went to sleep.

A long-haul drive and a night-owl talk made me sleep till noon. I set out to enjoy a nice bath in the nearby waterfall. The hills were freezing chill in the shiny morning.

An ice-cold furious waterfall bath filled me with freshness. The natural water-massaging-therapy and herbal aroma had added bliss to my aura.

After a relaxed bath, I returned to my room. A delightful brunch was set already there; I had it tummy full. I thanked Abhi for the hospitality.

A beautiful balcony was attached to the room. I stepped onto it. There was a breath-taking lake view in front. No human voice, no noise and no music, nothing but enhanced landscape. My soul and mind were completely blank. I stood still, let time breeze away and reinvigorate me. Falling steep waters, lavishing leaves and my soul – all had a heart-to-heart talk.

The nature therapy rebooted my brain, I was ready to start afresh.

Tossed the story pad, notepads and pen over the table, I rested on the cushion couch in the balcony edge.

Any new thoughts, keynotes, atypical words that can be used, situations I come across and scenes that I feel good to be added to a story, all I used to record in the notepad. Once a chain of thoughts were linked into decent shape and a story line farmed, I'd write them down in my story pad as chapters.

Typewriting or digital typing, that's not my thing. I prefer to hand write to put my thoughts in a flow. After completing each chapter, I'd convert them into the digital version and share with Mannu for review.

Pulling out a fresh note pad, I started filling the steady stream of thoughts, character names, situations, and other stuff that crowded my mind.

The mornings I spent mostly brainstorming and writing notes; my afternoons were for a nap; during the evenings, I used to hear music and walk around the town to feel good fresh air; post dinner was devoted to watching outstanding romantic movies and reading exceptional love novels. Simple but functional routine.

Mannu also looked for a beautiful love plot from Chennai. She strongly believed I would develop any plot into a fine story; her last one-year journey with the amateur author and his sincere efforts to breed his first novel gave her that confidence.

~~~

Getting bored of the resort food, I planned to munch on some spicy evening snacks. I walked to the bustling area of the town.

Collating the thoughts took a couple of weeks. However, I did not end up circling an impressive plot.

'Shit...movies and novels didn't spark any romance in mind,' I felt exhausted as I walked.

Tom questioned me, 'Should romance spark in the mind or heart?'

'Damn, I don't know...,' I said. We laughed.

On the way, I crossed the park that I'd regularly pass by whenever I walked to town. A busy park filled with lovers, honeymoon couples, and topped with few married and elderly folks; it was a lively garden.

Tom came up with a weird idea, 'How about you ask these lovers or couples about their love life?'

'Seriously?'

'Yeah, perhaps a hint for the story line or at least it can aid in some portions of the chapters,' he added a caution too, 'Act sensibly though.'

'Not bad...' I said, gathered confidence and entered the park, thrilled for some real-time love stories.

Scanned the people around, I closed my eyes and let my instinct choose one.

It did; a young couple – the guy in jeans and t-shirt and the girl in skinny jeans and checked shirt.

'Hey...'I approached them gaining some guts.

'Hi, do we know each other?' he confused.

'No... but I want to...' I said and explained the reason for my interference in their love date.

They both looked at each other confused.

'Weird it is, huh? I know. On a fine evening, some random guy walks in and asks about your love life for his story, it should be. Okay, how about this, you need not tell me your name or where are you from. I just need to know how you both fell for each other,' I finished.

'You are weird, yes, but not scary...' she smiled and started, 'we first met in a book fair.'

Both pitched in to continue their sweet how-we-fell-for-each-other story and completed. I had no time to note down, so I recorded the whole conversation with their consent.

'Thank you so much, it really means a lot...' I said and took off.

'Thrilling, isn't it?' I said within.

Tom tipped off, 'Damn yes...lucky that you got into good hands.'

Every evening from then, I walked into park, randomly picked a couple, and gave them my reason of interruption. A few agreed and most refused. Some ignored me like a worm. Not all couples were lovers or love marriage, there were a few arranged marriage couples who shared their after-marriage love-life, which was equally delightful.

The next few days passed well with a lot of real-time stories.

~~~

'Thank you so much, *ka*,' I thanked the maid in the resort and walked out.

Desperate search yielded versatile thoughts. All those strenuous efforts helped me a lot to admire love. It did blossom many new feelings within me but still they failed to induce an impressive plot; I ended up filling my notepads, rather ink-straining my story pad.

After spending a good amount of time in hills, I realized that nothing turned good. I bid 'Hasta-la-vista' to Javadhu hills and wheeled off to Chennai. Not with a story but with lots of notes and thoughts.

All Izz Well

The sun slid below the horizon; dusk welcomed me to Chennai. I parked the car and entered home smiling at my mom. She had prepared a yummy dinner and was waiting for my arrival as I had informed her before starting from the hills.

'Five minutes,' I gestured at her and went straight into my room to fresh up.

Weeks later, I walked into the clumsy room, my very own realm. Whatever mood I'd be in, returning to home was always bliss. I tossed my backpack on the bed.

The laptop from the bag peeped out. Transformed itself into a lap-machine it treaded towards me.

'Power me up, chief. You haven't checked Facebook, YouTube or blogs for days now,' it invited.

'Not interested, my Jarvis,' I said. Down in the mouth, it deformed to the laptop and took back its place.

'Life will be superb if these things happen for real,' I said.

Tom said, 'Science Fiction is part of your DNA.' We laughed at the funny imagination.

Really, I was too tired to update any status or check any social-network. I went into the washroom, took a hot bath and wiped my worries about the story off my face.

Put on casuals, I came out to the dining table.

'*Enna pa*, you look dull?' mom asked. Moms have an extraordinary power to read their child's mind; bare face, wet or in whatever state it could be. Every mom's superpower, it is.

'Nothing...' I answered.

'How's the new story?' she asked along serving food on our plates.

'Going good, *ma*, I am about to finalize a plot. Soon I will develop it into a story,' I fake-pacified her.

Mom was quite aware of my day-to-day life. After I chose writing over my IT career, few discussions would bring up a heat conversation between my dad and me, but my mom was always supportive.

Initially, she was the one who worried a lot but she later understood how badly I aspired to be an author and stood by my side. My dad did understand as well but concerns about my future stopped him from fully accepting the idea.

Mom and I had an enjoyable time during dinner. I briefed her about my experience of hills and she gave me a lowdown about neighbors and relatives.

After dinner, I picked my backpack and took off immediately for Mannu's home.

The minute I reached Chennai, I thought to go straight to her home, but I didn't want my mom to skip her dinner time. Mannu and I would beat our gums, I knew, if we start to chat after a break.

We stayed just a couple of kilometres apart in OMR, Chennai. After my dad had retired, my parents had moved to Chennai and stayed with me. However, a year after they'd moved in I'd resigned my job and got fully involved in writing. They'd started compelling me to leave Chennai so that we could move to our native. I was not interested in moving from Chennai nor leaving Mannu.

After a 20 minute-walk, I reached Mannu's home. I grabbed the chocolate box out and put the backpack on the dining table. I sneaked into her room and shouted, '*Machi...*'

'Heyyyyyyyy,' she pushed her specs overhead and screamed, 'Stupid, can't you answer my calls or messages, it's been since a week we spoke.'

Habitually, I ignore cellphone when I am out for writing. Though many a times Mannu has requested not to, I won't listen. We're used to it; I'd repeat my folly and anger her and she'd bite my head off every time.

'Chill, *di*, it is not new,' I sat next to her in the bed to console.

She pushed me down and kicked, 'Change yourself, God...you can't be the same fool.'

'Okay, okay, cool. See, I brought you homemade chocolates.'

'Oh, you think these chocolates are gonna save you? No way,' she started chasing me. We ran around the room, then hall and at last settled on the chairs next to the dining table.

Both of us broke into laughter for a while and gulped for air.

Chewing the chocolates, she asked, 'How was the hills?'

'Awesome! Incredibly beautiful days. Abhi and I had a great chat after a long time. The stay in the cottage was outstanding; they served delicious food. The hills, climate and scenery all were perfect,' I continued and narrated the entire trip to her.

About an hour, I took to describe the travel.

She sat before me and heard it wholly, like a small kid, crunching off half box of chocolates. However, I consciously skipped my failure of getting a new story.

'Sooooooper,' she excitedly gave a buddy-pat on my shoulder and asked, 'Then, come to the story. Where are you on finding one love story?' she asked.

'Yeah, I almost closed one...' I paused.

'Oh...' she looked up straight in my eyes and asked 'no, you didn't. Did you?' she caught me there.

'No. I am stuck where I was. Fuck the trip,' my dejected face was revealed. I failed to fake-pacify her.

She changed the topic, 'We should have fallen in love. You'd have written that as a story,' she teased.

'Huh…great,' I smiled.

'Seriously, hills, movies, novels and real-life stories, nothing helped you?'

'Nope. They all helped to gather many feelings but not an impactful plot; I'm still squeezing my brain hard to build a base plot. Stories, hill station, nature and loneliness – all ditched me. I fell over at the very first hurdle,' my frustration ferried out.

'See, that's why I ask you to talk to me regularly. You sounded upset when you last spoke to me from there. You have to relax, *da*.'

'No, Mannu. I can't. You were right, I am a vegetable,' I said. I pulled my backpack, grabbed the notepad and mobile phone out and flung them over the dining table and said, 'See the notes and hear the recordings.'

Came to my feet, I moved near the window and continued with humiliation, 'I couldn't build a character, an instance or nothing. Check the story pad, not a single word written. It is absolutely empty, as plain and blank as me.'

'Guru, please. Give it some time. Things will work out. All of a sudden a love story won't happen,' she stood up.

'Agreed, no need of a story, how about a plot line, a character or at the least one situation?' agony flooded in my words, 'Nothing! I was twiddling my thumbs for more than a year over the first story, and now I am struggling much harder for a fresh start,' I paused and screamed, 'Fuck, my life is dead as a doornail.'

Till that moment, I never realized that frustration would hit me hard. Yes, I was bothered when I left the hills, but I certainly didn't see this coming. I broke down as I couldn't hold my pain within.

Mannu came near, 'Are you crying? *Enna da*? please stop,' she wiped my tears off.

'I couldn't hold this. I couldn't...' I wept hard. My hands started shivering.

Grabbed my right hand tight, she said, 'You're gonna finalize a story line. Very soon it will happen. Stop worrying. Pease, please stop crying, *da*, I'd never seen you like this. Whatever happens, I am there for you...'

'No...' I started to speak. She hugged me.

We both stood still. It was first time Mannu had hugged me; for that matter of fact, that was the first time a girl hugged me. I didn't know how I should react. Should I stand still? Or push her away? Or should I embrace? I was confused.

Tom shouted from inside, 'Perverted moron, she is your best friend.'

'I'm just confused, didn't intend to embrace,' I countered within.

'She hasn't seen me overcome with grief and frustration. She didn't know what to do so she has hugged me,' Tom and myself concluded.

After a while, myself and Mannu moved away. We didn't utter a single word.

Time passed by.

To avoid any further embarrassment, I initiated the conversation, 'It's already late, mom will be waiting for me; I should start,' I blabbered with no sense. She knew I had my dinner and mom would've slept by then.

'Please, never ever repeat this. I will kill you,' she stuck up and shouted. She continued, 'Don't lose confidence. All izz well, *da*,' she rubbed my left cheek.

'Okay, don't embarrass me by talking about it. Don't you dare tell anyone I cried,' with one hand I rubbed my tears off and with the other, I picked the knife from table to warn her.

Both of us laughed.

'You do it again, I'll kick your ass,' she held heat.

'I dropped by to say Hi and to give chocolates. You made me feel bad.'

Mannu asked, 'Hey, I almost forgot. How's your one-sided headache?'

'Climate change, fewer sleeps and restless days, all added fuel to the fire. I couldn't concentrate properly because of the ache. I should soon consult a doctor.'

She kept mum.

'What?'

'You know that I had a similar pain. I took a pill which gave me a lot of relief. I forgot the name. Wait, I will search for it,' she went into her room.

In minutes, she came out with a capsule.

'Did you consult a doctor or you bought it from a pharmacy?' I asked.

'Hey, I got it after a proper doctor consultation. Try it. If it is not helping, then we will consult a doctor.'

Picking the water bottle from the dining table, I quickly gulped down the capsule.

'Okay, bye.'

'Hmmm... all things will settle soon. Everything is happening for something good. Sleep well, tomorrow we will catch up. Good night. Sweet dreams' she said and walked me out.

'Okay, Swamy Mandhakini, as you say,' I mocked her.

'Don't do it...' she said and we laughed.

'Don't finish all the chocolates, keep few for Keerthi.'

'No. I won't,' she shouted as I walked on street. We giggled .

After midnight, I returned home. Both mom and dad had slept. I tiptoed to my room, making no sound and closed the door quietly.

Hoping for a good sleep, I jumped onto the bed. Thoughts flashing in my mind was disturbing me. That day was unlike any other usual day. Not in ages, I was that thoroughly depressed or my cheeks were drenched in tears. My dearest friend had hugged me and shown a next-level care; that wasn't any usual day.

We had no intentions to do so, But I couldn't stop the new hormones thriving within me, which all those hills, lonely trip, movies, novels, and real-time stories failed to do.

Plugged in the earphones, I shut my eyes tight to stop the thought from growing any wilder. Perhaps to enter a good night and sweet dreams, as Mannu wished.

Head Over Heels

Screeching tires touch the runway and gives off dense smoke and odour. The Air India – Boeing 777 lands on the Delhi Indira Gandhi International Airport. 'Welcome to India,' the bold letters on the sign board, invites all passengers from London.

Handing over the arrival form to a beautiful air hostess, I come out of the plane and step on Indian land. After four years, I'm returning to India; busy schedule had kept me occupied. However, this journey doesn't end here, I must catch a connecting flight to reach my hometown, Chennai.

'Which way please for Chennai flight?' I ask an airport security officer, standing near the entrance door.

'Flight is delayed by 2 hours, sir,' he points his forefinger to a speaker. An announcement by a firm lady tone confirms it.

'Whaaaat? Should I wait for another 4 hours to reach my home? No way,' groaning within, I walk towards the waiting lounge.

Many people rush into the lounge to find a spot for them. I do, too. Scanning all around the room, I find a corner cushion couch. I stride to catch hold of that seat. I sit and rest my back.

Pulling my laptop out of the leather sleeve, I check my inbox for emails. After few minutes, I am done and put down the laptop. I walk to a nearby shop and get a chocolate, return to my seat, and start munching it. Now I just have to kill the remaining wait time.

Random English pop music booms via headphones in my ears as my eyes look around. People spread across the lounge; an old male walking his wife out, a young couple romancing in one corner, a group of young lads in conversation on the other corner and more people here and there in silo.

At the northern corner of the room, I see a lady playing with a girl kid. In her rosy pink frock, chubby cheeks and cute little hair fringes, she resembles a cute little angel. Her parents, sitting next to her, is laughing at her antics.

'Hiiiii....', I wave at the kid. She responds with a cute smile. That lady playing with the girl notices it and she stretches her neck to see me.

She is no lady nor girl, but one aged between both. 'Eyes are the window to soul'; her eyes are a preview of her incredible beauty. As we lock eyes, I swear everything around me slows down. I am in awe of her looks; it just hypnotizes me. White shirt and blue denim expose her every shape in the exact same way how it is.

Falling head over heels in love is a mirage, I have always thought. No, it isn't, I realize at that frac-sec.

The next song, a Tamil romantic score, plays in my headphones; whatta sweet coincidence. The composer is in his extreme in the love song that echoes in my head now. Whatever song you may listen to, when it comes to romance, only a native musical can give you that entirety. It uplifts my darn guts to stare further at her, ignoring the entire world around.

A glance-smile, she tosses at me and turns sideward. I end up seeing her right face profile. A strand of hair around her ear, mesmeric eyes, cute smile and perfect shape – all provokes a mysterious force within, which pulls me towards her.

Where does she live? What does she do? What language does she speak? I know nothing about her, but one hunch makes me confident. She waits in the same lounge, much like us who are waiting for the delayed flight to Chennai. And that precisely adds some more hours, so I can talk. At best, I have got the next couple of hours to stare at this pretty face. I laugh within.

'It is waste of time to think all this; somehow I should get her number,' I decide within and start walking towards her. My last few years of foreign upbringing gives me the courage to approach any stranger.

We are sitting diagonally opposite to each other. For first time ever in my life crossing this short stretch feels like a high-wire walk. An odd new feel is throbbing inside me. Perhaps, it is because I am standing in my very own home country or the thrill of talking to this unknown girl.

As I walk, she turns her neck towards me and gives a quick glimpse and turns back. Girls are quick and keen; they do not need a romantic music or a long gaze. A quick glance is all they need to read a guy from top to bottom. What analyses their mind do and what reactions they feel no human can ever discern.

Finally, I reach next to her and take the lucky seat that just got vacant. I say, 'Excuse me.'

She turns, looks at my eyes and says, 'Yes.'

'Are you waiting for the Chennai flight?' I start a sob conversation. I know that this is not a great pickup line.

She is about to talk but the announcement interrupts. 'All passengers waiting for Chennai flight can please board at Terminal 3,' a female voice irritates me.

'Seriously?' I almost slip it out, hearing the announcement.

She rises to her feet and walks towards Terminal 3. I wait on the same seat. She turns back and nods her head for a 'Yes' to answer my question with the same cute smile on her face.

That moment, my heart tumbles out and pumps a love rhythm. Her smile plays a mash up of love songs in my head. I literally wish to jump out of chair to shout 'Yes.' Realizing it is an airport and that I've hardly had a conversation with her, I control myself.

Recalling the romantic scenes and first meeting dialogues of many romantic movies, I collect my belongings and pace towards Terminal 3.

Rolling from the bed, I fell on the floor. 'What the fuck? What a dream it is,' I shouted. I checked the time, its 3:18 early in the morning. 'Why this dream, who is that girl? I haven't seen her once in my life? And who is he?' I asked within.

All those questions pulsating in my mind forced me to share the dream straightaway to someone. Who else? Mannu was the one I had.

The next moment I called Mannu. She didn't pick up. 'Hey, its 3 in the morning, who the hell will pick up,' Tom scolded me in half sleep.

Again and again those faces flashed in front of me. I badly wanted to know what happened when they both boarded the flight. How that guy would have took it up with her or he just flirted with her? Those unanswered questions left me awake the whole morning.

Gave Rise To…

Eyes wide-opened in shock, Mannu heard the whole dream that I narrated to her in a single breath.

'Is it a dream or first scene of your story? Oh... My... God... how can you remember a dream with all these details?' she raised her eyebrows in awe. Mannu was still on bed under her duvet in her nightdress. I ran to her in the morning to catch her and relieve myself out of the shock.

'Damn, it is a dream. Like it's not an ordinary dream, I can still feel it,' I said. Sitting next to her I rose to my feet and continued pacing, 'The girl in the dream...she is just awesome. Her figure, looks and charming grey eyes, she was perfect and so was that guy. Not just them, I can remember every person whom I've seen in that dream. That guy in the dream was me, I don't really know who she is.'

'You mean you?' Mannu asked.

'Hmmm... technically yes. Psychically he is not me. Slim, tall and handsome, he looked charismatic. Blazers, high-tech gadget and leather stuff, he looked rich too.'

'*Unakku enna da*? You are handsome too,' she comforted.

'Real handsome, I mean. He was like a ramp-walk model. In slim-fit shirt, his physique looked perfect. See me, I'm always a regular fit guy who desires to wear a slim fit once in lifetime,' I giggled.

'How you are describing him, how do you know he was slim and handsome? While detailing the dream, you didn't say anything about how you had seen yourself.'

'Dear Sherlock, you are correct. I forgot to say about that. When I was admiring her beauty, I mean he was. He didn't want to miss her. So, he took a selfie in his mobile, fitting her in the frame. That's how I know about his fancy gadget and physique.'

'Superb! You look for the dream girl. He is all mine,' she laughed.

'In truth, I couldn't take her off from my head; every now and then her face is flashing around,' I added and smiled.

'See, how much you are blushing...Leave that, have you ever seen her?'

'No, I haven't seen her anywhere. I thought she could be some film actress whom I have forgotten. Nope, she isn't one. From the morning, I really am trying hard to recall,' I said excitedlu.

'We will find, don't worry, *da*.'

'Have you ever come across this kinda weird feeling? You don't know your name, age, and the purpose of travel. No bloody idea of your past and future. Why you intend to go somewhere? "Chennai" here,' I double quoted on air and continued, 'nothing you know. After all, it is not a memory loss case,' I sighed.

'Are you crazy? It was just a dream. Dreams need no logic. You don't even need a flight, you can fly, literally, on your own to Chennai or even to Mars for that matter,' she consoled.

'Yeah, I get it. But then...' I stopped walking and sat on the chair opposite to the bed. I continued, 'but then, this dream is disturbing me a lot; any other hasn't done this to me. Who are they? What do they do? Why do they meet at the airport? and what really could have happened after they boarded the flight? All these questions are on a hyperloop in my mind. Like you asked, this could be my story's first scene. Perhaps, I do need answers for these questions. Else I should develop one.'

'You are so obsessed about this whole dream stuff. Ok, first let me freshen up, then I will help you research on the dream and related articles, which can help you in some way to recall it better.'

'I can recite the whole dream again, that's not what I'm looking for. All I need to know is their past and future,' I added.

'Yeah, yeah, I understand,' she said and came out of the duvet, and continued while making her bed, 'I will cover that too. Let's figure out a way to connect the dream and its instances, which might help in one or another way.'

'Out of all the chaos, making your bed is necessary now?'

Didn't utter a single word until she made her bed.Then, she turned towards me and said, 'Every morning, I prove myself that "I am in control of my life" by starting the day with making my bed. And have you never heard of this saying, "How you do anything is how you do everything"? I strongly believe in it.'

'Wow...that's Mannu,' I sarcastically smiled and clapped.

'You will realize it...Ok, give me 10 mins...I will freshen up. Then we shall look deep into your dream.' She went into the washroom.

That's in fact is Mannu. She is perfect and the exact opposite version of me.

Tom said, 'Not just first, making the bed is not even your last act of any day.' I laughed within.

After a few minutes, she came out all energized.

'Coffee?' she asked. I nodded a 'Yes.' She grabbed her specs and mobile and walked into the kitchen. I went to the balcony and sat on the swing.

That dream did impress me a lot and kindled my nerves to develop a script around it. I split the dream into scenes, noted down the sequences in my handbook and related different scenes out of the dream against my real life. The first scene was the Delhi airport where the flight landed from London. Second, he waited for the Chennai flight. Third, he worked on his emails. Later he met and admired the lady. And finally, they walked towards the boarding gate.

'I must be related to any one of these scenes,' I said within.

'Yessss...Yes,' I realized it within seconds and shouted for joy.

Once, I'd been to London while working for my previous employer; indeed, a delightful year of my life. I'd got a chance to travel to various places in and around England. A new country, new faces and new places truly had given me new thrills of life. I'd had a plenty of leisure time to explore new things. And most of all, I had the chance to read many books, which hypnotically inspired me and eventually inculcated the passion for writing in my mind.

At the end of that exquisite one year, I'd took a flight to India, which landed in Delhi, and connected to Chennai.

The only possibility for me to land in Delhi was that. Although, those costly gadgets on him had nothing to do with me. Also, that girl and those people in the airport and waiting lounge, I'd never seen them before.

Mannu came sat next to me on the bean bag. She brought a jam bottle, toasted breads and two mugs full of coffee placed on top of her closed laptop.

Pulled the wooden teapoy from the corner towards us, I helped her keep the breakfast down.

'What are you doing?' she asked while spreading jam on toasts.

'I took a crack to recall the dream.'

Tom said, 'No dude, you were recalling your London days.'

'I mean recalling those days in London, after which I landed in Delhi, like the guy in the dream...' I added.

'I won't forget those days...' Mannu said and handed a toast to me.

'What? Why?' I curiously asked.

'No...I mean, we didn't see each other for a year, like physically...'

'True.'

Mannu throwed her specs on, opened her laptop and said, 'Ok Ok, let's come back to our business. This article calls out detailed simple steps. For example: one simple step is to divide a dream into scenes and analyze the scenes.'

'Bravo,' I shouted.

'What?'

'That's exactly what I was trying till now,' I laughed.

'Genius *da nee*...' she giggled and continued, 'ok, read further, you should draw out even small things that you could have ignored.'

'Small things? I don't get you.'

'Wait...' she said texting someone in her mobile.

'Mannu, what small things?' I stressed.

'Hmmm...wait,' she continued texting.

'What you are doing?'

'Nothing, *da*...My client that doctor guy, Varun. We need to decide upon an important finance decision for his upcoming stock investment. I am trying to set up a meeting.'

'If you are busy, we can do this dream research stuff later.'

'No, I ammmmmmm dooooone,' she dragged along texting and put away her mobile. Mannu said, 'Let's focus. Where were we? Hmmm...Yeah, Small things. Hey, come on, you said that you handed over the arrival form to the air hostess, right?'

'Yes.'

'Obviously, you would have written your name in that form?'

'Hey yeah, the dream started from there, I did hand over the arrival form to that beautiful air hostess when the flight landed,' I said and handed her a jam-spreaded toast.

'Huh, to recall every instance, you need a girl in it, you have become filthy,' she fake-yelled.

'What's wrong in that?' I raised my eyebrows at her.

'Nothing, I better go and do my work. You enjoy remembering each girl in the dream,' she stood up.

'Hey, I am just teasing around. Ok, let's continue, I really do need to gain something out of this dream,' I comforted Mannu.

'Stupid, then concentrate on the dream' she sat down and continued, 'try remembering the name that you wrote.'

'Better let me note down all the clues you say, so later we shall reconsider one by one.'

'Next, your passport. It must have your photo, name, and address?' she asked.

'Nope, he might have had it in his waist pocket.'

'Next, he was checking the emails in the waiting lounge. What was that about? Any email related to profession or any useful information you remember?'

'Not even a single word, I remember no email, names, nothing,' I sighed.

'Hmmm...ok next...'

Bread served us breakfast. The feel of that dream gave rise to new hopes and pushed me forward to pursue more about dreams. We killed half a day in exploring stuffs about dream and skipped lunch.

However, we didn't end our research there. That afternoon we walked to a local library, explored a handful of books and read more about dreams.

After collating all our thoughts, insights, and learning, we discussed in detail the notes and scenes made from the dream.

'Is it 6:30 already?' Mannu asked.

'Yeah...we have wandered enough through the dreams. Let's start,' I said.

On the way we stopped at a chat-spot and enjoyed a delicious dinner. We started walking towards my home.

''Nothing working out...', my words sounded dull.

'Don't start all negative, *da*. Think, you got a reason to learn something new about dreams...' Mannu consoled.

'Hmmm, true that. But we didn't intend for it. If I could have found a way to make it through the characters of my dream, it should have helped me to develop a plot.'

Tom interrupted, 'You have failed to learn their life. How about you create one?'

Instantly, I smiled wide and said within, 'Fuck yeah, I mean you are correct.'

'What?' Mannu asked, seeing me smile suddenly.

'Nothing...you are correct...I really got a chance to explore something new...' I said and added, 'Thanks.'

'For?'

'For everything. For standing by me, helping me, struggling along and for walking me home.'

We reached my home.

She said, 'Someone seems really happy after a long time.'

'Yes, I am. May be because of the beautiful girl whom I saw in the dream...' I pulled Mannu's leg.

'Hahaha, comedy...'

'Or perhaps I've got a nice scene to start with my new story.'

'What? Really, you decided?' she got all enthusiastic.

'Yes, it triggers quite a stir whenever I rethink that airport scene. So why not stick to it and continue the story from there? Yes. I am gonna start my new love story,' I announced.

'Verrryyyy happy for you...' Mannu shouted.

She wished me all the luck and took off for her home.

That dream helped me regain my lost hopes. I went to bed that night awaiting my second story's kick off.

However, I did not realize what came next.

Missed You

Chapter 2:

Between a dark grey and a black suit my mind is on the fence about choosing one. A black limousine is waiting outside to pick me; I grab the black suit. The gel has set well on my hair, I comb it perfectly down and check myself in the mirror. From the fragrance bottles collection, I pick my favorite and spray it all over myself. Today is a momentous day; I take time to suit up. Turn front and back, I double-check myself on the mirror. All set.

Running down the stairs, I stride through hallway and reach the front entrance. Chauffeur, in his white safari, comes forward to open the passenger door of the car. Signaling 'no thanks,' I open and get on. Manoj boards after me. We hit the road.

We are on our way to attend the press conference arranged in a resort in East Coast Road (ECR) – Chennai. In fact, this conference is the very reason that pulled me down to Chennai from London.

After a long-haul journey, I reached Chennai yesterday evening, cancelled all due appointments and went straight to home from the airport, and slept soundly. A tireless mind is all I wished to attend this meet today.

Born and brought up here in Chennai, I knew that the best and quick way to a chill ride is ECR; the seaside drive is always refreshing and delighting. It will never fail to revitalize and enable anyone to enjoy the road journey with nature at its best.

Adoring the scenery, I don't wanna overlook myself and mess up the meet. I grab my phone and glimpse the notes for my speech. I don't usually warm up too much for any business meeting, product launch or public event and love to talk my heart out. However, this isn't any other usual meet; it is rather a sensitive and vital meet that demands me to organize myself and my words.

Done with revising the notes, I tap on the 'home' icon. The wallpaper on the screen draws my attention. A selfie focused not on me but her; I zoomed into to her face and set it as my wallpaper. From yesterday, this girl's cute smile and magnetic eyes are driving me crazy and bumping me off from inside.

The pleasant drive in the luxury limo along the picturesque road and her pretty face, all together evoke a new feel. The breezy sea-wind touched me over the closed window; the roadside trees dance in slow-motion.

Quickly, I take the iPad and iPencil out and start to draw the moment of our first meet at the airport. As I sketch, all my thoughts take me back to the place itself – Delhi airport.

~~~

'Are you also waiting for the Chennai flight?' I started a sob conversation.

She was about to talk but then an announcement interrupted. 'All passengers waiting for Chennai flight, please report at Terminal 3.'

'Seriously?' I almost slipped it out hearing the announcement.

She rose to her feet and walked towards Terminal 3. I still waited on the same seat. She turned back and nodded her head for a 'Yes,' to answer my question; same cute smile on her face.

That moment, my heart tumbled out and pumped a love rhythm. Her smile played a mash up of love songs in my head. I literally wished to jump out of chair and shout 'Yes.' Realizing it is an airport and hardly I conversed with her, I controlled myself.

Recalling romantic scenes and first-meeting dialogues of many romantic movies, I too paced towards Terminal 3.

My phone rang and stopped me.

'Good morning, Sir,' a male voice on the other side.

'Yes, may I know who this is?' I replied in a hurry, with no time to acknowledge his morning wishes.

'I'm Manoj, Sir, your personal assistant for this India visit,' he said.

'Personal assistant?' my voice raised up.

'Yes, Sir. Rahul, your personal assistant from London, appointed me to assist you.'

'I am gonna kill that Rahul,' I said to myself. On the phone I said, 'Okay, tell me. And this call better be of some importance.'

'I am waiting at the arrival gate to pick you up, Sir.'

'What?' I shouted. She was almost gone by then.

'I know you are about to board the Chennai flight, but sorry, Sir, there is a slight change in schedule. The President of India wants to meet and greet you in person before he leaves India this afternoon for an official visit,' he interrupted and completed in one breath.

'No, I have to catch the flight right now,' I replied in urge to cut the call, without listening to him.

'I am deeply sorry to bother you at this moment, Sir. Rahul and I were trying to reach you to inform this, but we couldn't. Even our emails bounced back.'

'Yes, my mailbox was full; I cleaned it up only a while ago.'

'The President was about to travel this morning, he postponed his meetings till the afternoon so he can accommodate your meeting, Sir.'

'You are making me feel bad. I don't want India's first citizen to wait for this individual,' I replied after I clearly heard him saying 'President.'

'Sorry to hear this, Sir. Perhaps it will be a quick meeting. After that a private plane will be standing by to fly you to Chennai. I request you to kindly reconsider.'

'Fine, but please don't embarrass me with this kind of treatment. A regular flight should do,' I said.

'As a backup, a business class seat is reserved in the afternoon flight, Sir.'

'So, you fixed the appointment?' I was angry.

'No, Sir, I'm extremely sorry to make you feel this way. I didn't conclude but was waiting for your confirmation.'

'Which gate you...'

'International Arrival Gate, Sir,' he cut in.

As a sad sack, I look out at Terminal 3. Almost all the passengers were on board. The final call was made for me. Everyone heard only my name as they repeated it loudly.

Put on the spot, I left the plane behind and so my dear girl, who just welcomed me with a warm smile.

'I should have walked with her to Terminal 3 and boarded the flight. It's totally my fault, I've missed her. No, it's not my fault; it is all because of this Rahul. Did I ask for an assistant for this quick trip, can't I manage on my own? An assistant should be an assistant; I clearly told him I don't want anyone, neither to assist nor to track my appointments. When I see him next, I will kill that guy,' I bawled within as I reached the International Arrival gate.

~~~

'Sir, we are almost here,' Manoj voice pulls me back into the car from Delhi airport.

That one phone call from this guy ruined all my plans to get acquainted with her. Now I don't know who she is and where she is from. Will we meet again? I don't know.

The final touches on the out-of-focus people around us finishes the sketch; it's focused on myself and her, the backgrounds and people are blurred out.

'Manoj, I shared a sketch with you. Get me the whereabouts of that girl.'

'Yes, Sir. I am on it,' he acknowledged.

The iPad goes down and my sight turns towards the window; I watch the roadside to distract my thoughts from her.

A race bike emitting fire crosses us; literally it does emit fire and stuns me for a sec.

'In this day and age, they race in ECR?' I ask.

'Not often, Sir. Here and there, yes, some crazy people do,' Manoj say.

Each time when I see people doing crazy things like this in name of fantasy, I wonder what excites them to road-race? Why can't they get that thrill in a racetrack? Why don't they realize that it's dangerous to rash drive along with domestic vehicles?

At last, we reach the resort where the press conference is set up. A grand flower arch is erected on the road entrance. A red carpet is stretched out from road till the resort entrance. Perhaps, till the Hall entrance.

All invitees, national and international media are gathered. A photo session is dedicated near the Hall entrance; all cameras flash away for a while.

We all enter the hall.

 ~~~

Wings of Dream

Chapter 3:

Amidst unceasing applauses, we all enter the hall.

Gathered crowd stands in unison. The anchor, standing behind the podium over the gorgeously draped dais, speaks, 'Good morning everyone. I feel elated and thrilled to welcome you all. Let's put our hands together to welcome the Ministry of Culture – India, Minister for Information Technology – India, Chief Minister of Tamil Nadu, all the business tycoons, and the star of today's occasion Mr Rajendra Raja,' she completes and smiles at me.

She steps off the dais and walks towards us to hand over flower bouquets. She walks me and other dignitaries to the stage. The baroque-chairs and a lengthy table, topped by name boards against each chair and water bottles, are placed in the dais hub. All the Central and State Ministers take their respective seats, leaving myself amidst them.

Political bigwigs, dignitaries, artistes and business magnates are seated facing the dais in round tables. The press, media, and thousands of online and social media folks are congregated behind them.

People are settling down in their respective seats. The anchor shows up to the podium again and continues her welcome speech, 'This is an exceedingly rare occasion, perhaps not just an occasion, a historical event indeed. We, from 'Eve' groups, feel honoured and overwhelmed to organize such an historical event. We welcome you all once again. More than welcome, I wish to congratulate and thank Mr Raj with a loud applause,' the hall reverberates instantly by applauses.

'All of you who have gathered here would already know of his achievements. Here is a small AV as a tribute or a humble token of our appreciation,' she says.

Lights dim in the auditorium and a video plays on the mega screen hanging from the ceiling on both the sides of the stage.

A narration goes over my photos scrolling as visuals, 'Born in Chennai, he completed his Bachelor of Arts in Government College of Fine Arts, Chennai. Later, he traveled overseas to complete his Master of Fine Arts from Oxford University, England. Painting chose him; he's proved himself as an eminent artist. The next decade – the digital era started booming, he gravitated towards digital art and co-founded 'Pixel Systems' – a leading transcontinental computer software company – headquartered in London, aligned towards multimedia and digital arts software development.

Amongst busy business days, his thirst towards arts made him fill his leisure times in hand-paintings.

One of such works made him the first Asian, and obviously the very first Indian, to win the International Contemporary Arts award in London.

Many of his significant works are world renowned and have occupied many art galleries across oceans. His award-winning masterpiece of art, 'Lan Cho' is now being considered for the *Guinness Book of World Records*. That work was auctioned for $926 Million USD, which is the highest price ever paid for a work of art till date.'

The AV ends and lights are back on. The crowd fills in with their constant ovation.

The host speaks, 'We are all gathered here to celebrate the very historical achievement and to thank Mr Raj. He astonished every Indian when he made his announcement, "I dedicate this art to every rural Indian kid, and donate this whole auction money for the development of their education". He did not stop by just saying it, he proved his words by forming the *"We 1"* foundation; it manages the funding of the auction money and makes sure his vision reaches the needy Indian kids.' The crowd's unceasing applauses start again.

She continues, 'We all know the trend of brain drain over the past decade. Many intellectuals and top scholars of leading educational institutions from India are migrating to foreign countries to familiarize this globe to new and different dimensions of technology. Mr Raj decided to bug this trend with his announcement during his quarterly meet last week. "A dedicated R&D center will be laid out in India. Though inventions are emerging from different countries, many inventors are Indians. Instead taking out those brains from their native place, I am approaching the flip side", he said. As per his desire, both the *We 1* foundation and the R&D center will be established and operated from Chennai – his birthplace.

The facts speak for themselves; he made all of us – Indians proud. He proved himself a prodigy, successful tycoon and most generous philanthropist. Our Indian government has organized this conference as a vote of thanks to acknowledge his achievements and to hear more about his vision. Thank you once again Mr Raj for being such an inspiration. The hall is all yours now,' she completes and steps aside the podium.

The hall quaked with a thunderous ovation when I come to my feet and walk towards the podium.

'You know what my favorite word is? The word "*Vanakkam*" when it addresses you all!', crowd cheers.

'A very great morning everyone! I sincerely welcome all the dignitaries on stage and off stage, and my friends who have gathered here from all walks of life. Thank you so very much for gathering here. Thanks for the AV and your kind words, Ma'am. An exaggeration it is to say I have created a masterpiece and to address me a philanthropist,' I say and look at her. She acknowledges with a polite smile.

'There are diverse legends out there; they are more than just artists. Here I am, an amateur who is looking for every viable way to become an artist,' crowd interrupts with disapproval with noooo and ooh sounds. I laugh, move away from the podium, take the mic in hand, and bow before the crowd, acknowledging their love.

'Let's skip out talks of me. I much appreciate all your time and on interest of it, let me jump into the purpose of this gathering,' I say, step off the dais and walk amongst the mass.

'It is boring to stand on the dais, delivering a speech or answering your questions.' Crowd giggles.

'I am Raj and you all just now heard a short biography of mine in the name of brief,' hall fills with laughs again. 'The sole purpose of my visit to India is this conference, but the sole purpose of this meet is neither to blow my own trumpet nor about my arts. I really do need all your support to make our vision even bigger, make it reach every denied poor kid across India.

Not alone I stepped forward, many of my friends, business partners, clients and they in turn spread the request to their circle, to come forward and join hands together. All these resources must be directed via a proper channel and be transparent to all who supported it. After lot of discussions, 'We 1' foundation was formed. Till date, we raised a humungous amount of $3 Billion USD in a net and it's growing,' a loud applause interrupted and prevailed for a while.

'Through the *We 1* foundation, various charitable deeds have been planned in different areas. The first vision is "Wings of Dreams", named after Dr APJ Abdul Kalam Sir's book *Wings of Fire*. This vision is dedicated to our beloved Kalam sir. I sincerely believe in his words, "Let us sacrifice our today so that our children can have a better tomorrow", which is in fact the root for this vision – education for all.' Applauses rises to the roof.

'I had a privilege of meeting Kalam sir; we had an energetic conversation for couple of hours. He asked all about me and my family, my urge for art and about my future. I took that occasion to detail him about my thoughts on this vision. He felt incredibly happy, "Your passion to make rural India reach out, makes me feel happy. Your wish to give a chance to necessitous children is remarkable. I wish you all success", he said.' Applauses all over again.

'The word "chance" which he said during that conversation did drive me sane. Many struggles these kids and youths go through to get a chance for achieving what they deserve. Through *We 1* we thrive to make that possible and serve them chances to explore and attempt it,' before I finish applauses fill in.

'Finally, the R&D center; I am much delighted to announce the launch of 'FOIK.' No 'U' and 'C.' It is 'F' 'O' 'I' 'K',' I spell each letter and give a pause.' Laughs and murmurs, here and there.

'Calm down. Calm down. Let me finish it. FOIK, meaning, "First Of Its Kind", is the R&D center, to be launched in India, dedicated to new innovations on the digital arts and image processing. This exclusive center will use only Indian brains to invent products, develop and deliver it from India. This dedicated center will be a birthplace for many other companies, but it will not have any direct or indirect business relation with Pixel Systems. That means India's very own international digital product companies are on their way. Along the money we raised till now, every quarter a percentage of profit from Pixel Systems and from the newborn companies will be funded into *We 1* foundation.' Clapping and smiling everywhere.

'Many plans are laid out to make these visions come true, which you can access through web portals and social media pages. All the references and the details are mentioned in the pamphlets in your hand. Do visit and subscribe to those pages and share it throughout the nation; your word of mouth can go a long way. We've requested for a full front page publish about our vision, *'We 1'* foundation and 'FOIK' in all the daily newspaper. We are discussing with media, news channels and few YouTubers for programs on this front. I hope and wish this to be a news ever in Indian history, after our independence, which will get released in all language newspapers and channels tomorrow. I thank all of you for your support and I am sure you will lead us way ahead towards the fortune of these visions. Now the hall is over to you.' I complete and open the Q&A forum.

After a ceaseless loud applause, a guy from the south corner of the hall, comes up with the first question, 'Congratulations for your award, Sir. Do you believe that you reached your lifetime achievement?'

'Thank you, Sir, for breaking the ice' I smile and continue, 'I would say yes and a no. Once I thought hard work and dedication will make you successful. But then, I realized I must work even harder than yesterday to taste the real fruit that is tomorrow's success. So, it is both yes and no,' loud applauses follow.

'Why and what inspired you to contribute the whole bid money and start this campaign?' a girl from the middle asks.

'Me, myself. Yes, it is all about me. I am very selfish, and I always think about me,' I give a pause. The hall goes in silence. I continue, 'The hard days I faced during my early ages to fulfill my needs forced me to take this step. I know there are many out there who haven't got their chance yet. I ask them to be selfish in achieving their own dreams and to help out others in being selfish too,' I laugh, and the audience follows with a loud clapping again.

'You feel that you have won your dreams?' a guy from left corner raises his voice.

'For me dreams are like waves, they are infinite and so is winning it. I am dreaming newly every day. Working to surf along them,' I say.

Session continued with many interesting questions about 'We 1's' vision, my upcoming paintings, Pixel systems' future and 'FOIK.' The ministers voiced their thanks notes and their ideology over 'We 1' and 'FOIK,' in between the QEA section. We were all done and about to wind up.

'One last question sir, perhaps a controversy, I would say. What is your stand on the talks saying that you have a personal intention behind the scenes for these initiatives?' I hear a voice from the right corner.

'Yes...', I turn to answer the question but I am stunned seeing her. She is the one, the same girl who'd made me go crazy for the past couple of days. I can't believe my eyes. She looks more beautiful in this off-shoulder grey taupe dolman top and steel blue denim; more magnetic and perfect than that day when I first met her in airport. My eyes are stuck on her; I fail to react and stand still for a moment.

'Before answering this question, may I know your name?' I gain my conscious back and ask intentionally and curiously with an unintentional look. However, my feelings burst out as blush in my face. So, does she.

'Ms Shelly,' she says.

Miss, I note it. Is it an intentional hint for me or is it casual? I start studying her milieu with the name in a frac-sec.

'Yes, I have a personal intention behind the scenes. My personal intention is nothing other than that my brothers and sisters of my own nation, my family should cross the poverty barriers and must make a career that they aspire for,' I confidently reply.

She doesn't seem to disagree, instead she claps and so does the whole gathering.

Yet, I can't take my eyes off her. I get on the dais, take my seat and start staring at her.

The inauguration of '*We 1*' foundation and 'FOIK' kicked off after the QEA session, followed by thanking speech of some more bigwigs. Truly, I wish to listen to them, but I couldn't. How could I have overlooked her before, I scold myself. The event came to an end. Every now and then we both shared a look. Her eyes, as always, keep mesmerizing me.

All of us gather once more for a quick photo-shoot. People start leaving the hall. The ministers and I are escorted to our cars by the guards. I bid bye and thanks to all and come near my car. Manoj, the driver, and I board the car.

'Hold on... start only after I say,' I command.

My eyes are stuck to her; she walks towards a van, and hands over the stuff she has held and goes to the parking area. She is busy in talking with the people around.

Manoj iterates the due appointments for the day one by one; I am least bothered to it. Nothing reaches my sense right now. Eagerly, I wait for her to start.

She walks to the bike parking, wears a leather overcoat, kneecaps, and helmet. She ignites her bike and passes us in a quick second. I hardly recognize her crossing us. I am knocked down by a feather now. It's her on that bike, the very same race bike that crossed us in the morning on ECR.

'Please follow that bike,' I say in a hurry to the driver.

'Yes, Sir, I will try to speed up,' he says with a mystified look and starts the limo. I understand that look. There is no way to follow her. She is nowhere near when we start.

She is a reporter, which surprises me. More than that, she rides a race bike. I can't believe all these are happening. Not all girls are racers and a reporter, no offense to the media personnel, but still. I can't digest that my lovely girl is both. I lean towards the window; confusion fills me.

'Manoj, can you repeat once again the day's appointments?' I ask so I can divert myself. But no, I fail. She and her thoughts are filled in me now.

…In Deep Water

Chapter 4:

Whatta pin-drop silence! Once in a blue moon, I'll be amidst nothing but a warmth silence; busy days and busier people do not grant me the privilege of peace. The water is blue, warm and calm. As I get close by, the warm breeze lashes me. I strip myself off from the heavy robe into jammers, dive into the pool and break the fence of silence. Splish-splashing the water, I swim across.

As I swim, the water strews away, much like my mind that met Ms Shelly again. This time not as any lovely girl, but as a reporter, more than that as a racer.

Yesterday was completely packed. I slept pretty late, but then her thoughts kept buzzing around and threw me out of the bed early in the morning. Thus, I've decided to swim.

Hold back the pace, I free-strike across as quiet as a flying owl. The water in the pool regained its lost silence.

~~~

After the press conference, yesterday, I landed in a cultural fest organized in my alma mater. Our principal is close to my heart, he had asked for my presence.

High school students organized the fete to honor their alumnus and to felicitate different art forms. A bunch of events were set forth to entertain; colourful dance shows, kids painting display and a brief stage play was performed to portray how art transforms life.

However, no space was left in my mind to be amused . Perhaps, it was in a total chaos; Shelly was racing somewhere at the back of my mind.

My face did index the mind. My Principal noticed my anxiety and asked, 'You look very vexed today, is something bothering you?'

'No, Sir, nothing at all. I'm good.'

'No, you aren't. I know you, Raj, this isn't you.'

Yes, I was truly not. She had threw me off. I floated on the clouds at the instant we met again, nevertheless meeting her in the real 'her' had pulled me deep down. Why did I meet her? Do I really need her in my life? All those questions made me ruminate more and more.

No words I found that could explain my trouble, so I filled the space with a smile and nod.

'You are a gifted kid; I've seen you through all times and will continue too. Whatever it may be that worries you, soon things will fall in your hands. Keep them at bay and enjoy the show. See these children play, you will forget whatever it could be,' he said.

For a second, his counsel words turned back time and took us back to school days. We smiled and turned towards the stage.

'Fish bite more readily when seas are rough; perception matters and it takes advantage of any situation,' a kid said this dialogue to his mate as they were nearing the play's climax.

The coincidence made me laugh. 'Yes, perception does matter,' I said within.

At the end, I addressed the fellow children with a concise speech, as my principal requested. Until dusk, I spent time with those adorable and talented kids. I tried all possible ways to be attentive, to honor their love, but she didn't let me. Every now and then her face and thoughts overwhelmed me. I bid goodbye and took leave.

Then, we arrived at a night party arranged by Indian business kingpins and service providers. Talk and sign; Booze and dance; discussion and celebration went hand in hand. Few crucial decisions were made on the FOIK front and the upcoming projects.

Just before dawn we wrapped up. I came back to my beach-suite-house in ECR. The tiredness pushed me to sleep, but her face kept raging in my mind. From the moment we met in the conference, she seems to have gained control of me. Things I see, people I talk with, discussions I made, and in every breath I took, she filled herself in.

~~~

Swim across infinite, I try exhaust myself out of her. Luck does not favor me, she wins again; I can't make out the tremor moment in which I saw her report in a race bike.

Naught to go bad with reporters; I never thought my knots will go around a girl with a collar mic. Well, whenever I think about any reporter, the only thing that strikes my mind is questions. How can they come up with all these spontaneous questions? Always surprises me. I can't imagine a life that loaded full of question marks. Her biking adds oil to the furious engine. What a cinematic combo she is – a reporter on a race bike. Any incident in town, she will whizz report there in a second.

All deem race through my mind faster than her bike could. Tonight, I am traveling back to London; just one day more to choose between lives, one, which I live in now as cool as I wish or the other, hold tight to back seat of the zippy bike and answer all her creaky questions.

Swim across few more laps, I rest at the Jacuzzi corner of the pool.

This house and especially this pool has seen me more than my parents did in the past decade. Whenever I visit Chennai, whatsoever tight my schedule be, at the least an hour I will free myself to swim here.

The swimming pool, the garden around, and my gorgeous suite house, inch by inch all the details I'd hand-drawn-designed and had made sure, to be built well stuck to it. Close to the core are my house and this pool.

Coincidence or perhaps destiny; many crucial decisions of my life have been taken here. It could be the warm silence surrounded or the intense water that energized my senses to think straight and act precise. Many career-changing decisions have been made at this very place. Now it turns to be my life at spot. It's the call time on her; should I continue to draw my life crowning her a Queen or should I throw her out to sentence? Could I really throw her away?

'Darn these feelings,' I cry out. True that love hurts. Strangely, in my case love does symptom hate even before it starts and lands me in deep water.

My phone rings and cuts in my agitation. The ringtone echoes through the water and sounds louder than usual. I swim across fast to answer.

'Hello! Am I speaking with Mr Raj?' a female voice on the other side.

'Yes, speaking.'

'Good morning! Sorry to disturb you in the morning, Sir,' she says in a sweet voice.

'May I know who this is?'

'I am Shelly; we met yesterday at the conference.'

Yeah, she it is. I am dumbstruck after realizing it's none other than my zippy-racer girl. I don't want to show the shock; I instead act ignorant. 'Shelly?'

'Remember me, Sir?'

'How can I forget, you are killing me from inside,' I want to yell out loud, but I hide within and respond modestly, 'Yes, I do. You are the one who last questioned me, right?'

I can hear a laugh on the other side, 'Yes, Sir, please tell me.'

Her voice is no lesser than herself, mellifluous it is. 'No, Raj, not again, hold sturdy.' I caution to myself.

But wait, what should I tell? I ask her, 'Sorry, I don't get you?'

'Your person came here to my office, gave your personal number and asked me to ring you.'

What the heck? Why will anyone do that? I control my tongue and ask as far as politely I can, 'May I know who gave my number?'

'Manoj, he introduced himself, if I am not wrong.'

That name infuriates me. Again, seriously? Is he gone off his rocker? He was the one who stopped me off boarding the flight with her. Now he gave my number and asked her to call. Wouldn't she misunderstand me? Yes, she would. Sure, she would have minded.

When we started from the conference and in-between somewhere on our chase after her, I had said, 'Good if we catch hold of her and I get a chance to talk to her.' He should have taken that literally. Manoj held himself back for some marketing and promotion works and didn't join me for the school fest. He should have sneaked in that gap to meet her.

What shall I say, how will I face her?

'Sir, are you there?'

'Yeah, yes,' my words tremble.

'Please tell me, Sir,' she repeats.

'I really didn't mean to make you call me. He missed the point, forgive me. But it is true that I need to talk to you. Rather not on call, shall we meet for a coffee?' I gain some nerve and ask.

'If you allow me to ask, may I know if it's related to any personal interview or promotional video for your campaign? So, I may come with my crew?' she wonders.

'No, no, please no. It's nothing to do with that. I need to meet you in person, just as Shelly not a reporter.'

Did she really forget? I am the one who stared at her in the airport and nearly approached her, or is she acting ignorant?

'Oh, ok sir. Where shall we meet?'

'Call me Raj, please.'

'Ok sir...' she starts but changes, 'Ok Raj, where shall we meet?'

'ECR coffee shop at 10:30, fine?'

'Yep, that works.'

'You will get the address in text. Bye, see you.'

'Bye.' She hangs up.

The next moment I ring Manoj and start yelling, 'Are you out of mind?' I tell him what have just happened.

'Please don't jump to conclusions, Sir, hear me once.' He continues to console me. 'I learnt on the way back from Delhi that I was the reason why you were unable to speak with Madam. I really wish to make things right between you both. So, I took the liberty to hand your number over to Madam and made sure you are not missing her again.'

'But Manoj, I really didn't mean to make her call me. Do you understand that?' my voice loses anger.

'I really am sorry, Sir, shall I...' he starts. I cut in and say, 'No, please, it is not a problem. Leave it.' I hang up realizing that there is no point in shouting at him.

Somehow, I've grown confidence to ask her out for coffee, but now I am in two minds. Why should we meet? What am I gonna tell her? Should I really continue this relation? Her influence, even before our relationship, makes question marks revolve around me.

Shelly has again gloriously given me the chills. I jump out of the pool and rush up for the first date; only to decide whether it is a date or not? What an irony, isn't it?

...To Pull The Rabbit Out of Hat

Busy traffic halted all moving vehicles and jammed my car somewhere in-between.

'Are you done?' I asked Mannu who sat beside me.

She didn't respond but kept to the reading. The iPad's screen reflected as a Micro-copy in her specs. Her curious eyeballs swung along forth and back to peruse each sentence word by word and wrapped her up amid the chapters.

'Madam?'

'Yeah, yeah, I am here, *da*. Keep your eyes on the road and hold the peace,' she said. I did so.

After driving three quarters of distance, she finally finished reading and locked the screen.

'How's it?' Words screamed out forthwith; curiosity for the first review turned me into a school kid who waits for term's result.

She widened a big smile to relax me; a convinced smile out of Mannu is no easy feat, in fact her forthright criticism had backed me up in completing my first book with utmost satisfaction.

Mannu took her specs off and said, 'Very good and unique narration, *da*, keep it up. Really, anyone who reads this story won't believe it's from a debutant. I loved every bit of it and thoroughly enjoyed it. It's a fabulous start,' she scored me outstanding.

'I trust that you are bound to our agreement to be genuine by your review and not to utter appeasing words'.

'Hey, no way. That's not gonna do any good for you. I'm an open critic of your work. You can trust me, rockstar,' she patted my back.

Both laughed in unison.

'I feel a lot relived now. Really, I was tense waiting to hear your comments,' I exhaled.

'You've pitch-perfectly expressed his feelings for her and his anxiety on knowing the real her; not many stories focus on this kinda complex relations, that's a plus. It's indeed a well start and I wish the same through the end,' she added compliments.

'But Mannu, you have to be more specific with your reviews this time. Not just a reader or critic, you must act like a content editor. After reading, talk about how the scenes made you feel, whether the narrative was interesting and how the language can be strengthened to staple more intensity. So...' I paused.

'So?'

'So, I've decided to choose someone else to be a reader.'

'Oh, you decided. Hmmm, will you at least let me know who it is?' anger shadowed her words.

'Seriously, Mannu?'

'What?'

'Are you mad at me for including someone else into this?' traffic cleared out and made the way to hit the road; The car picked up pace and so did our conversation.

'God, no, no. Why would I be mad? It's your story, you can share it with anyone,' she spun around towards the windshield.

'Mannu, never turn your back on me. Listen to me.'

'I am listening,' she said, facing away.

'This genre, unlike the previous one, is not my cup of tea. Your mere comments might not suffice; I need your thorough backing. Then and there, I will share the chapters with you for reviewing and editing.'

She interrupted, 'Not only with me. With one more person too...'

'Just... first listen. We are one for this story; you can't contribute any objective view as you are too involved in the process. A fresh pair of eyes is must. Let us choose one to share – only "one",' I double-quoted on the air.

'Oh! Won't your story leak out now? You were quite adamant about not sharing your first story with anyone but now...'

'Yes, I was.' I cut in and continued, 'I worried sharing with someone would leak the story out. But now I don't have a choice.'

'You are fickle minded, Guru' she flipped out.

'Give it a rest, Mannu,' I screamed at her.

It'd been ages since we picked a quarrel. Both kept mum as I drove further.

'Sorry,' she broke out after minutes.

An instant smile on my face. But then I hid it in a corner and said, 'No, you needn't.'

'Okies, it's my bad,' she turned towards me and smiled.

'Peace,' I countered with a smile and continued, 'I totally agree with you. Yes, the story might slip out, so we need to find one who is near and trustworthy.'

'You do have one in your mind, don't you?'

'Not yet chosen, but...' I dragged.

'But what? Say it.'

'Keerthi.'

'Keerthi, Ahaan?'

'Not again,' I said within and started a convincing-mode talk, 'I've seen her many a times roaming all-round your home reading big-bound books. You said that every so often she will be engrossed in books and not that talkative kind. An approachable bookworm, she would fit the bill. What say?'

'So, you have decided?'

'Come on, dear.'

'Okay, what's next?'

'After completing a chapter, we will join hands to better it. Once we complete some sizable number of chapters, we shall roll that over to Keerthi. She can read and share her views, make sense?'

Mannu gave an agreeing smile.

'Ah. Yeah, this is the smile. This is my Mannu.'

In fact, that's what our cute relationship is all about; we might hit a rough patch now and then, but we'd cool down with a crack of smile. After that conversation, I realized that she was damn possessive over me.

'Now, share your innate reviews for the chapters,' I asked.

'Not now, we'll discuss later.'

We arrived. I parked the car in the designated lot before the clinic. In bold letters the board read "V Talk" – Psychotherapy Centre.'

'So, what's gonna happen when they meet in the café?' curiously Mannu asked as we walked in. I said nothing but smiled.

Tom said, ' Ask her to wait until tomorrow.'

'It's not funny. That's why we are here. Shut up please, my lovely conscience,' I shushed him.

We walked to the front desk. The receptionist was busily talking on the phone.

'Excuse me,' I said.

'One minute,' she said on the phone, closed the mic in one hand and asked, 'Welcome, Sir. May I help you?'

'We have an appointment,' I said. 'With Dr Varun,' Mannu added.

She checked the PC monitor and glanced the wall clock; it held its hands straight apart to show 6 pm. 'You are on time; please walk straight, take the second right and wait in the room,' she directed us with an Pan-Am smile and returned to her phone conversation.

We led ourselves in and sat there.

After a couple of minutes, 'Hi Mannu, how are you?' a voice came from the back.

A man in his 30s, stood beside. We came to our feet and acknowledged with a smile.

'You should be Guru? I can totally see him in his eyes,' he laughed and shook hands with me.

'How are you, Varun?' Mannu shook hands with him.

'I am good. You look gorgeous in orange,' he said.

She giggled and replied, 'Oh! thank you. It's just casuals.'

'Come on in,' he walked towards his room. We followed.

I said within, 'Seriously?'

Tom laughed at me, 'Easy for them to catch the pulse. Not like you, duffer.'

'He is irritating,' I yelled within.

'Gorgeous he says, and you laugh? Where is that coming from?' I murmured in Mannu's left ear as we walked.

'Oh boy! Someone seems jealous?' she murmured and smiled.

'No one is,' I stepped away.

'Sweet darling, this is called socializing,' she pacified me.

We entered the counseling room.

Varun said, 'Please, settle down.'

We took our seats on the smiley yellow bean bags laid in the middle of the room. That room took me by surprise; nowhere had it resembled a psychologist's counselling room. No clichéd table and chairs nor any medical equipment; rather it was intensified with elegance wave.

Walls were blown up with a landscape portraying the sun shining in between a dense forest. Trees and branches were themed to resemble brain waves. One of the tree branches stretched to the roof in the south corner. Sphere-shaped book racks dangled, alike fruits, in the branch.

His name "Varun Krishnan" was quilling-crafted by atypical font, affixed to a wooden stick, and stood two feet vertical in the adjacent corner. A big academic cap topped over it to hold a few rolled sheets hung around it. Later, I came to know those were his graduated degrees.

'Impressive! I may not hate this guy,' I said within.

Tom said, 'You really are indecisive.'

'You often let one fact slip; you are my conscience, try to act like one. His flirting talk did irritate me; indeed it could have come out for socializing,' I defied within.

Tom added, 'Whatever, he seems cool. Mannu got you strike the right key, wisely use it.'

We settled within, 'True that. I should have an open conversation.'

Lately, I was very confused and mentally stuck. Mannu came up with this psychotherapy consultation idea. At first, I was hesitant about consultation and stuffs, but then she forced me to go through one. Dr Varun was Mannu's client. She said she knows this guy well and he was cool to start with. She believed that he could pull the rabbit out of hat to crack my illusions down.

Varun initiated the talk, 'Mannu briefed the situation over phone. How is your brain talking now, Mr Guru?'

'Nothing but love,' I countered instantly; all three laughed. It broke the ice.

'Good, isn't it? Not all are blessed for that,' he laughed and said, 'Though Mannu briefed me, I wish to hear it from you.'

'Sure, before that can we please agree a few terms on papers?' I gestured Mannu to put the agreement bond papers on to him.

'Please take your time, Varun. Do go over all the terms before you sign,' Mannu said and handed the papers over.

'Hmmm, I did expect a confidential-talk-session, but signing bonds...you topped the cake with cherry,' he smiled.

'More than confidentiality, it's my future, so I believe you won't mind...' I asked.

'No, not at all. A word won't leave this room,' he gestured zipping up his mouth.

After a good amount of time, he finished reading all terms of the agreement detailed between the therapists and the client in evaluating therapy and its outcomes. We signed the papers.

Varun took a recorder out, pressed the red button and gestured me to start.

'Sure,' I started, 'For the past few days I was desperate to start a new story...' I stopped.

With a smile, I said, 'Alright, I'll first give you some history about me. I quit my IT career over writing. Spent a year and ended up with a sci-fi novel, which didn't impress any such publisher. Eventually, one of them was interested and liked my narration, but then they forced me to write a love story to kick up a debut hit.'

He cut in, 'Love is the mantra of success, people think.'

We grinned.

'Chasing behind a love story, I travelled places, studied feelings and did all means of search. All ended up with nothing and proved to be a wild goose chase. Throwing all away, I returned to Mannu. Unsurprisingly my oasis of hope consoled me with her whole heart,' I paused to turn towards Mannu. She gave her soothing smile.

'Then, that night I got this dream, where I, not as this me, but in more luxury me, landed in Delhi airport, met a girl, and fell in love. Next morning, I narrated the dream to Mannu; weirdly I remembered every detail of that dream.'

Varun cut in, 'Can you be clear on what you mean by details? Sorry to keep cutting in as you talk. I do so to better understand.'

'Never mind. Details, I mean every detail of that dream, from the dress colour till the words I heard around.'

'Okay, please continue.'

'That day Mannu and I discussed and explored a lot about that dream, but we arrived at nothing. Nevertheless, that dream rejuvenated me; when I was about to give up, it convinced me to continue. So, we reached an agreement to kick start my love story with that dream as my first chapter.' I paused and gulped a glass of water.

'Good going, continue,' Varun said.

'Yes, all were going good and normal till then' I stopped and looked at Mannu.

'Go ahead,' she mouthed.

'The next night I...I dreamt again... a continuance of that same dream.'

'Did it start exactly from where you left?' Varun curiously asked.

'No, it didn't, but the story continued.'

'Then...'

'Startled the next morning, I ran to Mannu to describe. She got shocked too; we looked for similar cases on the web but arrived at nothing. We came to our own conclusion that it's just because I was besotted with the first dream. Also decided to go off with it.'

'Hmmm! When did you decide that you need counselling?'

'Not then. Not until I dreamt again and again and again. The dreams didn't stop with just 2 days; every day from then I get dreams in which their story continues; almost a week has gone now. Every detail is clear cut in my mind when I wake up the next morning. I fell in love with these dreams and characters in it. The situations they revolve around took me aback. I fixed myself to write the dreams as a story, turned all those dreams into chapters and started a love story,' in one breathe I finally let it all out.

'Hmmm, quite interesting' Varun exclaimed.

'What really brought me here is that love for dreams. At first, I want to understand why these dreams, but now it's beyond that. I need these dreams to continue. Love towards the dream became my obsession, and my happiness has turned into worry. What if I didn't get the dream tonight? How will I continue the story? What if people come to know the story is borne out of dreams? These questions kill me from inside. Perhaps, in worst case if the dreams stop, I can add a pinch of fiction to continue and complete the story. However, it is injustice to the story, I think,' I put my face down.

'Not just obsession, Guru is mentally devastated,' Mannu exhaled and said, 'he should be normal to think better. So, I suggested a psychological consultation to understand what is happening and why are these dreams occurring.'

Varun heard us all out. Switched the recorder off, he put his thinking cap on. After a few minutes, he said, 'Progressive dreams.'

Mannu and I caught eyes in confusion.

...Hit It Off

Usually, I am punctual; alike any other meeting, I've made it on time to the café and waiting for a few minutes now. Amusment, thrill, anxity, and thousands of emotions trampoline in me. Ran behind profession and passion, I never had a chance to find a date for a date; technically this is my first.

An art-themed café – different art forms are on display all around this place. Vintage collections of classical music instruments like Veena, Sitar, Flute, Mridangam, and few others hung from ceiling. Kathak face, Bharatanatyam face and Kathakali face are embossed into rectangle canvases to pleasingly decorate the South wall.

The ECR glitters outside the entrance door, I've chose to sit facing the road. Adjacent to the door, a collage of pretty paintings is stuck to wall, symbolizing love. Paintings are always enthralling; they never fail to induce me to create one. However, these speak different language now. They compel me to just sense and reflect the love it holds. It breaks me into smile and takes me to the moment I first met Shelly, the moment when she mesmerizingly turned me red. Love makes people go crazy, I'm no different. It made me push all my busy plans and wait here smiling all alone; yet I adore it.

Time has passed by enjoying this aesthetic interior. Then, furiously a bike arrives to distract me.

Shelly, it is. She gets down, removes her leather jacket and gloves and places them over the bike. She takes the helmet off, losing her brunette hair out. Her hair spreads all over her face, gently, she wipes it off to reveal the glowing face in full; no much make up, it's pure and pretty as a picture. No artificial overdo costume but a simple tee and jeans. Pale red T-shirt with a printed silhouette girl face in center and bold white words reading 'My me,' and skinny blue faded denim. Figure-hugging top; she's really dressed to kill.

For God's sake, I've came in casual wear too; it would have been embarrassing to date in a blazer. Three-forth fold brown-blue checked shirt unbuttoned on top of a white V-neck tee and dark grey denim. I match her well.

She walks in gesturing 'Hi.' She comes close near the table, holds her ears with her hands, says 'Sorry, terrible traffic.'

Right away, I smile and come to my feet to shake hands. Gently, I hold her right hand. Not familiar with *desi*-dating etiquettes I refrain from a hug. Perhaps, I should have hugged her; a gentle-first-date-hug should've done magic.

She takes leave to washroom and makes me wait only for few more minutes. She returns and sits opposite. A quick touch of gloss on the lips and a light shade on the eyes. Yet, they add stones to the jewel.

'You look a lot lovelier than I remember,' a charging pickup line I stick to.

She acknowledges with a cool smile; she would have got it, this is not just a meet and greet. Or perhaps, she should be pretty much familiar with dating etiquettes.

Her sharp grey eyes look straight into mine; they are an instant hypnotizer, and her glossy lips pulls mine for a quick tap. Going crazy here, I realize to stop these thoughts before they grow any wilder, and I should start a conversation.

'Speak,' I scold myself.

'Yes sir, ouch forgot, yes Raj,' she starts instead. I smile.

'Here, I've come as nothing but Ms Shelly,' she giggles.

'You recognize me?' I open with a stupid question.

'You are a rockstar; the whole world knows you. How would I miss? You are on today's headlines and cover news. You are all over India, through Asia and some other parts of the world too,' Ms Shelly hides somewhere deep inside and lets the journalist speak for her now.

'Will you please answer as Ms Shelly. I mean to ask, do you recognize me in person?'

'Hmmm...how wouldn't I? Delhi airport, dark blazers, showy leather stuffs and a cool smile. Yes, I do remember.' She holds to that smile.

Waw waw waw...women are women; they really don't need a staring look. For a second, she looked at me, but then she recites inch to inch. My instinct kept echoing that she should also be fancying the Delhi airport meet for the past couple of days.

'Hmmm...' I express exclaim in face and say, 'I thought you didn't notice me.'

'Come on! Seriously? But I ignored you as I was mad at you,' she says with a fake hate. I enjoy the cute reaction on her face.

She continues, 'My vacation was ruined because of your sudden visit. Almost after a decade we visited Delhi; due to my father's work, we have settled in Chennai. All of a sudden the message came from office asking me to report back to Chennai within three days; two-week vacation went in vain.'

The instant she has said, 'settled in Chennai', I feel a stronger bond between us.

'Is it so? But I did not see any hate in your eyes that day. All I remember was a wide smile saying 'yes' before you walked into the terminal.'

'Yes, I was not pleased till that moment you came sit next to me. Some charisma calmed me down; you would have felt that more if you had boarded. But, you missed,' she over-talks to confirm herself that she expected me on-board.

Realizing it, she blushes.

'I couldn't board then; an important meeting held me in Delhi.'

'Yes, I came to know about that later.'

'But I really am so sorry...I didn't realize my India visit would ruin my dearie's vacation,' all of a sudden it comes out of me from nowhere.

We catch eyes with a second of silence and feel each other in our eyes. We speak nothing but silence. Right now, I don't care the biker her or question bank her, all I feel for is Ms Shelly; this indeed is a date.

'Brown suites you,' she distracts us.

'Thank you,' I acknowledge.

'You look simply...' she stops.

'Simply?'

'No, you are simply...simple, I mean. I have always seen you all wrapped up only in formal attires.' She finishes saying, 'You look simply stunning in casuals, if I have to be frank.'

Huh...it's a darn icebreaker, she opens. Both of us blush, now, wider.

'Shall I order something for you? Perhaps my favorite.'

'Sure. Shall I choose mine for you?'

'Please, you go first,' I push the menu towards her.

'Excuse me,' Shelly calls for the barista. She walks towards us from the counter and says, 'Yes Ma'am.'

'Caramel crunchy Frappe top it with whipped cream,' Shelly orders.

'Make it two,' I grin.

She leaves with the order. Shelly asks, 'Your favorite too?'

'No.'

She surprises, 'Then?'

'Let's not start with a bitter black hot coffee, I thought. So, I went with yours. We will surely stop by here on a rainy evening, so I left one favorite to order then.'

'Oh, leaving just one favorite is enough?' naughtily she counters. We grin.

'Here normally they take a while to serve,' she says.

'Oh! Ma'am is not new to this spot, it seems?'

'In fact, no. On leisure times, I take ECR bike rides, so my favorite stop-spot this is. Not a date-spot sir,' she gets what I meant and replies sweetly. She adds, 'You are not bad at questions either.'

'Oh boy, influential radiation is extremely near,' I counter. We laugh.

'Now your turn, shoot one' I point my right hand at her.

'Hmmm...how many London dates it took to end up here?'

I show '0' joining my right thumb and fore finger. 'The past decade was crucial, I weighed up nothing but building Pixel Systems'

'I believe we are true here' she smiles and says, 'your turn.'

'Only truth, else dare' I say, we laugh, and I ask, 'What came first in your mind when we met?'

'Here?'

'Yes.'

'Beware, Shelly, you are gonna fall a lot deeper than you thought.' Both laugh at the instant.

We take our turns from then to ask out our past; from the place of birth to last night dinner, we share in lively questions.

The chill coffee have reached our table and tasted our lips; caramel fails to taste sweet against our chat.

Again and again, I do fall for her. She is awesome. As sweet as her voice, she looks gorgeous, bold and ambitious. Her vision for the career is clear. Just the word 'perfect' will better describe our relation.

Time should stand still, I wish. No meetings, no travel and no foreign land; couple of more coffees and never-ending chat with this girl is all I yearn for, now.

'No, it's not gonna happen, not today,' the bike she has parked out, stares at me and speaks.

Yes, it's not. I should start soon. Evening, I have a flight to catch and millions of dollars worth of contracts are waiting my signature in a business meet before that.

Before we start, I wish I could gift her something... something to remember me, this day and this place; a special touch that stands for my feelings for her.

'I love your work. I am a huge fan of your "Fly Girl" modern art. But I feel you are less into art now-a-days. Not to be offensive, I sense somehow 'Pixels' took over the Artist Raj in you.'

My ears turned deaf and my eyes are wandering around to pick something to gift. My first gift to my girl; it should be memorable and not just a bouquet or chocolates or some stuffs.

As I look around, the wall paintings catch me. I think for a while and smile.

'What did you say?' I ask.

'I love your work.'

'No after that.'

'I sense somehow 'Pixels' took over the artist Raj in you,' she repeats.

Now, I smile wider. She's confused.

'Excuse me,' I call the barista. She comes next to the table. I pull her down and murmur to her ear. She thinks for a sec and says, 'Ok sir' and takes leave.

'What?'

'Wait a minute.'

Swiftly, she comes back to hand a plain paper and pen.

Shelly looks at me puzzled, I sign to calm down and give me some time. She takes her phone out and gets busy with it.

Fidgeting the pen in hand, I beat my brain out. Finally, I see in mind what I am looking for. I transmute it to the paper.

Quarter hour has passed by; with no more patience, Shelly asks, 'I can't wait, please tell me what it is?'

'A couple of more minutes.'

After 5 minutes, I am done. I call the same girl from counter and murmur to her again. She takes leave. Shelly politely watches the happenings around with the same pretty smile.

She comes back with a café gift bag in her hand. I collect it and thank her.

'Here you go,' I say and gift the bag to Shelly.

'Atleast tell me now, what it is?' she grabs the bag.

'A small gift from Raj, to remember this day.'

We giggle. She opens the bag. She looks more puzzled when she brings the paper out. Her reaction is close and stoic.

'It is something unusual, so please better tell what this is to my tiny brain,' she smiles.

'What you see?'

'I can see dots capped with numbers on a plain paper,' she flips the paper front and back.

'Connect the dots, as simple as that,' I tell her.

'Seriously, you want me to do this now?' she laughs.

'Yes. I am all free. Are you?'

'Of course, I am happy to do it,' she says, picks the pen from table and starts connecting the dots.

After good enough minutes, I ask her, 'Done?'

'Yes, almost done. Just 10 more dots, gonna finish, let's count down,' she says and counts loud as connecting the dots.

"9,' '8,' '7,' '6,' '5,' '4,' '3,' '2,' '1' and done' we say in unison.

'Wow' she shouts and reads out loud, 'Shelly.'

She continues, 'Looks like you have used a new font. All dots meet to reveal my name, is it?'

'Is that what you see? Hmmm...give it, let me look,' I pull the paper from her hand, across the table.

'Yeah, I see only "Shelly",' I point her on air and smile.

'No, I don't believe you,' she starts to say but shuts spellbound when I reverse and hand the paper over to her.

'Wow! Wow! Wow!' she cries out.

Smile stretches wide and her face is stuck in smiling.

'You like it?'

'Like it? I love it. I will treasure this...how can you? I'm taken aback...' she struggles to complete the lines.

'You deserve a standing ovation' she goes to her feet and claps.

'Hey, please sit down, you are embarrassing me,' I shush her. She sits holding her cute smile.

'How can you? Seriously I can't believe,' she repeats.

'A special gift to remember this day. Something which I'm,' I stop, shake head and say, 'Artist Raj is used to.'

'This is unbelievable. Wait a sec,' she pulls her phone out, clicks a selfie and compares. She continues, 'Perfect, both are alike. I didn't realize my face is hidden under the connected dots. You are genius and you are...you are just awesome,' she compliments.

Yes, it is. I hid her face under the name, in reverse. Years ago, I practiced an art-kind called Illusion Painting. That helped now. I've plotted the dots in a certain sequence to reveal her name but to hide her face. So, at first glance she couldn't recognize.

She looks happier than I've thought. Not just happy, she is awestruck.

We lock eyes and don't speak a word. She tears up.

'I need to leave,' she says.

'Oh...'

'Sorry, Raj, I forgot. I have to rush... for... a meeting...' she stammers.

Clearly, I read her lie and say, 'Thought we would spend some more time.'

'Yes, I love too...but...I should leave. Now.'

We come to our feet to shake a bye.

Shelly comes near, closely hugs me.

'Thank you so much, all this means a lot to me,' she leaves.

Something weird, perhaps a vibe, passes between us in that moment and in that hug.

She tries to hide but we totally hit it off.

We both have fell for each other, I realize and smile. Butterflies are all over me.

 ~~~

Flying Start

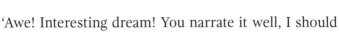

'Awe! Interesting dream! You narrate it well, I should say,' Varun smiled.

Twisting around the chair, he directed his assistant, 'Guru sounds clear. Resting pulse rate is in range, you shall remove the skin electrodes and pulse meter.'

She pulled me up from the stretcher bed and removed all the strings attached.

He continued, 'I know you are waiting to shoot a bunch of questions at me. Please hold on to that trigger for few more minutes. You shall go back to the counselling room and wait,' he said, swung around and continued the discussion further with his assistant in deep-medical terms, which sounded all Greek to me. I left the diagnosis center. Walked straight to the counselling room.

~~~

Previous night.

Varun heard us all out. Switched the recorder off, he put his thinking cap on. After few minutes, he said, 'Progressive dreams'

Mannu and I caught eyes in confusion.

'Don't go at sixes and sevens, I will explain more. Before that, I need to put Guru under study, to read his medicals, which will help us put the situation into right perspective,' Varun said.

'Medical tests?' I asked.

'Yes. You should undergo pre-diagnosis tests and your sleep should undergo observation.'

'I'm physically all good. It's just my anxiety,' I cut in.

'I totally get you; I am neither gonna throw you under surgery nor in ICU observation. Basic procedures to read your brain processes, how your body system functions and what your dreams make you, that's it,' he pulled his iPad out and started typing.

He turned the screen towards us and said, 'See, these are the tests that will be put on you. I start only after you agree.'

Mannu said, 'Diagnosis, tests and observations, anything is fine. God...I need this stupid to come out of this mental strain.'

'Are you sure? Tests and observations?' I mouthed at her.

'Shush, we will talk,' she gestured and said to Varun, 'you start the arrangements.'

'OK, then. We need to put him under study' he paused, checked his wristwatch, mind-calculated and said, 'now it is 7:00 pm, medicals and sleep-study will push it to early morning tomorrow. Is it fine for you folks or I can take an appointment tomorrow?'

'No no, we are totally fine,' Mannu said.

'You go home. Why you need to wait?' I asked.

'That's fine, *da. Konjam* work *iruku*, I've my laptop with me,' she said.

Varun picked the intercom, dialed and said to the receiver, 'Instructions have been sent, prepare the diagnosis room.' Then, he said to me, 'Guru, exactly 5 minutes, all will be set. If you want to use the rest room, it's outside to your left. When you are ready, walk into the big white door straight opposite; I will be waiting there.' He stepped out of the room.

'Are you serious, Mannu? Why all these tests and stuffs?' I asked her the next moment Varun left.

'Yes, I am. You need a break; you're badly stressed out because of these dreams, story and writing.'

'I am doing all this just for you,' I rose to my feet.

'Cool' she jumped and hi-fived.

After using the washroom, I walked to the washbasin, splashed water on my face and wiped it off. Looked straight into the mirror, I saw my face covered in beard, reflecting lifelessness.

'Fuck,' I screamed.

Tom said, 'Don't you worry so much. She is correct; we should come out of this. I can't hold the pressure.'

'Donno... I don't feel like doing all these therapist and diagnosis stuffs. I'm not that kinda guy,' I said within.

Tom added, 'Just relax and go with the flow.'

Nothing, I had to say. I stepped out.

Rang my mom, I throw a random lie at her for staying the night out. Then, I walked straight inside the Chamber-of-diagnosis.

~~~

Mannu was working on her laptop in the counselling room. Hearing my footsteps, she turned and asked, 'Hey, you alright? They didn't allow me inside, *da*.'

'Yeah, once I appeared, they put me inside a big white panel for an hour; some sort of scanning device, I guess. After that they moved me to a chamber-like panel to connect wires all over my head, few under eyes and others over my chest and asked me to sleep. That's all I remember. In the morning, Varun woke me up and enquired how I slept. Did I feel any disturbances? How well I dreamt? Was it like normal? blah blah blah questions...I answered all. Then he asked me to recite the dream. I did. After that, he asked me to wait here. He is discussing over the diagnoses results with his assistant,' I finished in one breath.

She didn't sleep, her fluffy eyes showed up. I asked Mannu, 'Can't you give some rest to yourself?'

'A critical work was due to finish, I was fully engaged in it,' she removed her specs and squeezed her tired eyes.

She checked the time on clock to say, 'Oh it's already 3:00, I didn't even realize.'

'Yeah, that's why I am asking,' I said.

'Leave it. First tell me what you dreamt? Did they meet in the café? What happened?' she curiously asked.

Readily, I replied, 'Yeah, they met, and you know something, she too has feelings for him...'

'I knew it,' Mannu excited.

Varun came inside saying, 'Hey folks, it's time for a little talk.'

We three sat down.

'I will tell you later,' I whispered at Mannu.

'"Gunan Rudhra", I like your name,' he read my full name in the report and smiled at me. He asked, 'You didn't feel much of a discomfort sleeping the night here, did you?'

'No. I'm fine. You should be probably asking Mannu,' I said.

Mannu cut in, 'Hey, no problem, I am all good.'

He held the smile to say, 'Good news! Results prove you are medically clear and we are good to focus only on psychoanalysis.'

Mannu and I caught us in a relieved smile. I asked, 'Then why these dreams?'

'Yes, I'm coming to that. You are undergoing a sequence of dreams that continue over a period of sleep cycles which is generally termed as progressive dreams.'

We expressed a puzzled face.

He spotted it, raised his hand to ask, 'Don't you get?'

We shook our heads a 'no.'

He continued, 'Answer this, what is A + B whole square?'

'A square + B square + 2AB,' we answered like the first bench school kids.

'Now think of a complex formula or a theory which you couldn't find an answer for hours until finally you fell asleep. And in your dream, you find an answer. Has anyone of you felt this kinda condition before?'

'Yes, I did. Not just once, a lot,' I said.

'There you go. While we are asleep, our subconscious mind continues to work on problems our conscious mind has failed to solve. You are now undergoing a similar situation. Progressive dream is a lengthy process; solution is in due course of dreams. One dream may continue where an earlier dream left off. Mostly these dreams are problem-solving, focused to explore different perceptions to a problem, situation or relationship. To put it in simple terms, whenever a dream is recurring our subconscious has something important to tell us; your dreams are trying to help you out to win your situation,' he smiled.

An agreeing smile was all I had then to respond.

'For that matter of fact, many scientific discoveries were made in dreams. To quote an example, you should know Dmitri Mendeleev, who discovered the periodic table.'

Mannu said, 'Hmmm.'

'But you know how he really did discover it?'

We shook a 'no' again.

He stood up, walked across the room and continued, 'Dmitri Mendeleev was obsessed with finding a logical way to organize the chemical elements. He wrote the element's names and its property on cards, one in each card. Mendeleev tried to figure out a sequence to arrange the cards for many hours. Eventually, he fell asleep at his desk. When he woke up, he was surprised. He found that his subconscious mind had done the work for him! He, in fact, mentioned it that, "In a dream I saw a table where all the elements fell into place as required. Awakening, I immediately wrote it down on a piece of paper".'

'Brilliant,' I said.

'True that the subconscious mind is immensely powerful. The conscious mind absorbs plenty of data while awake, while the subconscious mind can process and make more sense of the data while asleep.'

'So, my dreams are the solution for my desperateness over finding a love story?'

'Not literally, perhaps it could lay a path to the solution. Talking about dreams, I read your earlier dreams, I mean your chapters, but those sounded more like a story to me than dreams; They are difficult to interpret. That's when I asked you to tell your last night dream and again you narrated it more like a story' he chuckled.

'He is used to it,' Mannu smiled.

'That's good for a writer, but difficult for a psychotherapist' he smiled and continued, 'no worries. There are a lot of other means of diagnosing. During our course of sittings, we will discuss them in greater detail.'

'But...'I tried cutting in.

He didn't allow, 'Let me complete before you start with the questions. Your desperation over finding a love story might have triggered the dreams, but I won't arrive at any conclusions now.'

He concluded, 'I will end by clarifying a few things. First – to be frank with you, I can't assure these dreams will continue nor I will stop it from coming. No one can,' Varun smiled. 'My job is to make sure that you get rid of your obsessions over them. Second – I need to know more about your dreams to derive the pattern embedded; it could ease the exploration of blockaded spots. So, if the dream continues, keep sending them. And last – stick to this psychoanalysis schedule, nothing but it will help. That's it, I am done, now you shall...' he opened his hand.

'Can you do something to put this entire story as one dream in me? That will solve all my problems,' I innocently asked.

Laughing loudly, he asked, 'What Mannu, am I looking like Leonardo DiCaprio from *Inception*?'

We laughed.

Varun continued, 'No buddy, that's impossible. Hmmm, let me put it this way. The therapy sessions will make you least bothered to ask this question in future.'

'Am I doing the right thing? What if people come to know that the story is not mine but of my dreams?'

'Dreams are nothing but reflections of your subconscious, so technically this is your story. You are a good narrator, with or without dreams you will shine; no one can deny it,' he smiled.

'That's relieving to hear' I smiled back and asked, 'One last question, I have no connections to these dreams or characters in it or the places they go. Will I get a convincing answer for these?'

'Yeah, that's why I am asking you to share the dreams. I will work on that,' he said and added, 'Many times we feel that we remember a dream to its full, but that's not the reality. In most cases only 30% to 40% of dreams will stay in conscious memory, that too only for a short while. I will share with you a few tricks which should help you record your dreams more efficiently.'

'Yes, that should do and regarding sharing the dreams...' I started.

He cut in, 'I totally understand, I will bind to our agreement, your chapters won't leak. Free your worries,' he smiled.

Mannu said, 'Thank you, Varun. Thank you so much. Please take some rest. I know you were completely involved in the observations last night.'

'Sure, I will. It's very rare to consult this kinda case. It is a treat for me,' he exclaimed.

'Thank you, please make sure to not extend this treat much. End it soon,' I said and we three broke into a laugh.

'Noted! I emailed you the analysis schedule and here's a copy,' he handed over the printout.

'Oh. From tomorrow?' I asked.

'Yes, I got a meeting cancelled so I scheduled it for you. And after that, we will meet once a week.'

'Sure,' Mannu guaranteed. We shook hands to leave.

Walking out of the clinic, we got into the car and I started to drive.

'Tell me, is he worth a visit?' Mannu asked right away.

'He is good. It's just a start, let us see where it goes.'

'OK, now tell me what happened in the café?'

'Check your mobile; I am forwarding you the recording. I did record while narrating it to him' I said, messaged the recorded file and added, 'You will fall for Raj after you hear what he gifted Shelly.'

'That guy took a gift with him?' she excited.

'No, he instantly made one.'

'Right away, I'm gonna hear it,' she giggled and put her earphones on.

The drive was smooth back to home; the roads were clear in the wee hours of the morning, just like my mind that had got rid its cobwebs with Varun's confident talk.

Yes, the chapters were out my dreams, but from where did the dreams come? They really were reflections of my subconscious. Aren't they? Yes, they certainly were as rightfully Dr Varun said. That insight gave a new feel which I hadn't felt for the story before. I was full of joys of spring when I found that out.

My first story was my brainchild, I would always proudly tell Mannu. That kind of intact relation I never felt with the latter, not even after completing chapters. Someway Varun's talk made me feel like it's mine; not as a child but as my love, first love.

First love eternally holds a divine purity. For anyone, their first love would load tons and tons of pleasure, and so did mine. That moment, when I felt the story was my first love, it was a treasure of a moment in my life; I bonded myself way tighter with the story.

Clear thought and stronger bond of relation, what more one could expect to continue writing? I was no different. Already, the story had got off to a flying start.

That's what therapists do; they're good at recalibrating one's mind to bring the flying colours out. His compelling approach persuaded me to stick to the counselling schedule.

Boon or Curse

"Days after I met Shelly passed four; feelings she got more to pour.

Last evening, she surprised at airport; presented a selfie, stamped love-visa on my passport.

Both our faces pictured in selfie; alike me she also shot one in Delhi.

Till last-minute of boarding, she hung out; blissful chat left our hearts flung out.

Wi-Fi aided a Chat-full flight travel; first day of date turned a rom-novel.

Chennai departed me with a love warning; I landed in London this early morning.

Directed chauffeur 'steer to Thames'; iconic Sun rise pictured dazzling flames.

Held myself over there till Brunch; delightful talk took a cold plunge.

Reached home put myself under shower; wet face on the mirror resembled flower.

Life altogether shifted a difference; outset showed out in all preference.

Dull black blazer colored fancy fit; sturdy sedan transmuted luxuriant Convert.

Waysides to the office came out retroversion; brief miles travel felt excursion.

Duty urges concentrate meeting; phone vibrates indulge in texting.

Work lacks verve; she got herself through my nerve.

Crazy I become with no clue; smile on face stuck by glue."

– Lovey-Dovey Raj

'Really? You wrote it?' Shelly asks.

On my way back home, I read the poem to her on a video call. She hears it in a half sleep, in the middle of her night.

'Yes, in fact, my debut poetic lines,' I proclaim.

'Lovely, really cute,'she laughs.

'You gotta hear where exactly I wrote it?'

'Where?'

'In the Board of Director's financial meet.'

She breaks into unceasing laugh; with not much choices left, I too join her.

Our date-talk takes off into the moon-lit sky and wings free through the night.

My first sitting of the counselling session, I waited in the counselling room at the "V Talk" – Psychotherapy Centre. Loading the questions over the weird-acting-area of my brain, I held the trigger to shoot at Dr Varun.

'Evening, Guru, how are things?' Varun entered the room.

'Hi, Good... all good.'

We took our seats.

'Ok let's get started.' He pressed a button behind his right; the next moment a big digital timer counted down from 59:59 on the wall.

'Just so you know, all our sessions are recorded. Both audio and video,' Varun pointed the cameras and mics. 'I will share you a copy of the recordings and the notes after each session.'

'Thank you so much,' I agreed with a smile.

'Now, tell me, what you dreamt yesterday and how you feel about it?'

'Sure.'

Concisely, I recited the dream; a few minutes passed.

'Shelly was scared; she ran away from the café. Well, she could not hold her feelings for him for long. Thrilled I am that they are dating; the story did take a superb shape,' I finished.

Heard me all out, he sits silently for a minute. Then he handed an iPad and apple Pencil over, and said, 'Here, you hold. Recollect all the dreams you dreamt of till date and draw a doodle that comes to your mind.'

'Like a particular shape? Or any doodle that comes to mind?'

'Go free flow.'

Cracked a smiled at him, I took the iPad in hand. Closing my eyes, I ran a quick visual of all the dreams in my mind. Then, I started drawing crazy strokes.

Varun watched me closely as I drew. A few brief minutes passed. I completed and handed him over a messy scribbling; one should be beaten down to agree that's a doodle.

Grabbing the iPad, he made a few taps on its display. Boom...a high-definition 3D image projected instantly on the north corner of the room. That counseling room and Varun never ceased to amaze me in every visit.

Varun signaled, 'Let's walk.'

We walked near the projected doddle; it resembled beyond messy in the projection.

'Are you sure you recollected only the dreams but nothing else when you drew?'

'Of course, yes.'

'Thanks,' he smiled and continued. 'I've transferred and projected your digital drawing into a 3D hologram; it helps rationalizing details. Here you can see how the strokes interlink, how curvy they have stretched and these particle dots near the lines, they tell us how you sense your dreams.'

Varun zoomed into the inner structures of the drawings. He explained how my stress, anxiety, happiness and many more emotions were exposed through the strokes that formed the doodle structure; more anxiety resulted a complex structure.

Astonishingly, I stood still. A rich explanation followed his initial examination. My tiny brain processed the enormous data to make sense.

Shed light on what I should bother and what not, he didn't let me ask but already answered most of my questions, Dr Varun incredibly rocked.

'Beep...Beep...' timer sounded.

'We are done for today,' Varun circled the session 1 on in his iPad and added notes. He stopped and looked at me to ask, 'When did you get your first dream?'

'The night when I returned from Javadu hills, about a week ago.'

'You went to the hills to write a story, right? Did you make any notes?'

'Yes, I did. People I met, places I went and thoughts I had, I noted all of them down.'

'Do share those with me. Also, Mannu said you guys spent a full day decoding your first dream. Send me those notes as well, they can prove to be significant tools to dig deep into your dreams.'

'Definitely. So, we meet next week?'

'Yes, tag along to the schedule.'

'Should I narrate the whole week's dreams then or should I send it daily?'

'So, you're going to dream daily, you know that already?' sarcastically he smiled.

'What if?'

'How do you record the dreams now?'

'After I wake up in the morning, I write them down immediately and and at times I record it orally.'

'Provided the dreams continue, do me a favor, do not write. Record them and share it. Also, don't turn them into chapters until we meet next.'

'But...' I started. He cut in, 'Trust me, if you keep turning every dream into chapters, you are in soup.'

'I trust you,' I gave an acknowledging smile.

'Guru, please stick to the medications I prescribed. Any other questions you want to ask?'

'You answered those questions which I didn't even think through. Thank you so much.'

Varun smiled. We bid bye.

A relief ran through my nerves and spread a wide smile on my face. I walked out.

First thing first, I dialed Mannu's phone. Varun insisted not to bring anyone along. Any intervention might distract the very purpose of psychanalysis, he said.

'How it went, *da*?' Mannu on the other side.

'This guy is a fucking genius...' I cried out a typical swear-appreciation and continued to narrate the whole session on my drive back to home.

Quite late in the night, I reached home. Walked to my room, I changed into night wear and set myself straight to bed; clear mind and exhausted body pushed itself to deep sleep.

Sunlight sneaked through the window curtain and woke me up the next morning. I rolled on the bed in half sleep.

'Fuck yeah...' I shouted for joy when I came to conscious.

Next moment, I grabbed my phone, opened the recording app and pressed the Red recording button. I said, 'Dream 7. Shelly text-replied a heart eye emoji...'. I carried on and recorded the whole dream.

~~~

Session 2 – Varun checked me in and started the timer.

'A whole week of dream, huh?' Varun raised his eyebrows.

'Boon or curse, I am confused...'

'We will certainly figure it out,' put a smile out, Varun said. 'Walk with me.'

We came out of the counselling room. He took me into a different room; a high-tech lab with robotic machines engaged all over.

A giant artificially operated brain made from synthetic neurons was staged in the center. He lit the subconscious portion of the brain.

'I waited to see if the dreams continue before I intensely discuss about how the brain works to dream.' He smiled at me and continued, 'The neurons randomly fire verbal, visual and emotional motivations, the subconscious mind combines them into...Hmmm, how to put it?' he took a second to catch the word, 'Ha... a story-line; that's Dream. The subconscious mind stores both the conscious visuals we observe, and the unnoticed surroundings. During REM sleep...,' he carried on. Varun took a good amount of time to explain the different stages of sleep and many more dream theories.

'Why this lab?' I can't hold the built-up curiosity.

'Hahaha...' he laughed on the instant and asked, 'that's your first question after all?'

'No really, what about these robots? Why this brain?'

'Apart from medical and psychology, I was immensely gravitated towards Neurons. A PhD in Neuroscience and Nanomedicine it took to ably practice. My research projects are aimed at curing mental and emotional disorders.' He looked around, proclaimed, 'A dedicated tech lab is just a basic; advanced robot technology catalyzes the efforts.'

'Okay, let's get back to the counselling room,' Varun said.

Stunned at his wisdom, I followed him hypnotically.

Entered the counselling room, he said, 'About the notes you shared.'

'You cracked it, right? I know you would. So, who is this Shelly and Raj?' I cut in totally excited.

'No no, calm down. Hear me out. I created a Mind Map based on your dreams,' he stopped and questioned, 'You know Mind Maps?'

'Yeah. I created a few for my first story. It bettered the character development.'

'Sharp! Okay, in this Mind Map, I branched out the characters, their doings, locations and instances from the dreams. I found few coincidences with the notes.'

Varun projected the Mind Map. We went near and stopped.

'Raj landed in Delhi from London, this situation you came across in your own life a few years back.'

'Yes.'

He continued, 'Similarly, the first love couple you met in the Javadhu hills park, who shared their love story with you. They met in a book fair when that guy teased her for riding a muscular bike. Girl on bike – Shelly racing, I am sure you can relate. Next, your friend left in hurry the night you reached hills. He rushed to attend some business shot's press conference where State and Central Ministers and many big shots gathered. Mannu mentioned this when talking about your hills trip,' he paused and pointed the press conference chapter in the Map, 'Can you associate the root of the occurrence?'

'You are right.'

'Talking about their professions in relation to the hints from your notes...' Varun went on.

The deeper we ran down the mind map's branches, the farther we went unrevealing the hidden clues in the dream. He explained many more relations of mine to the dreams; few through my own life and few out of the lives from the notes.

Highlighting a few instances of the dreams, in fact 1 or 2 whole dreams as such, he interpreted how it is of no relation with the others. 'These portions or dreams might not turn out as a good chapter. They could water down the soul of your story,' he suggested.

Linking the nodes of the dream-chain, it made much more sense and proved that my very own subconscious part of the mind had developed a love story for me. At that moment, a train of confidence rushed through my blood to head. I was liberated as I felt like chief-in-command of what to take and what to leave out of the dreams.

The whole session was devoted on exploring the farthest ins and outs of the dreams.

We came back to our seats, Varun started typing down the notes for Session 2. I gulped down a full glass of water and the lot-to-process info.

'Fine, we'll meet next week. You got anything to say?' he asked.

'You are terrific,' I said in a reflex. Varun gestured a smile.

Punctually my conscience, Tom commented, 'Are you complementing him?'

'Yes, I do. Damn, awesome he is,' I replied within.

'Undoubtedly, he is,' Tom agreed.

Directly, I drove to Mannu's home.

'You gonna rewrite the story from the beginning?' Mannu raised her right hand and covered her face. The bright sun made her squint.

'No, not exactly. The first four chapters must be rethought...little tweaks here and there and the remaining dreams to be essence-extracted and converted into sizeable chapters.'

'Ok, *da*, it is too bright and hot out here. Let's go inside.'

'My favorite place, Mannu. This sit-out is like a lucky charm...let's decide this here.'

'You get your free tan. God, I don't wanna get fried...' she walked to her room.

'Hey wait...' I followed her.

'Mudiyala, *da*, I can't stand in the sun for a long time. Periods...second day.'

'Oh, first you sit down. Here...' I pulled the chair from the corner.

'Ok *da*...what exactly do I have to do? I can spend like 2 or 3 hours with you a day, max.' She exhaled, 'These days, after I start accepting corporate clients, I'm busy as a bee...'

'Good for you.'

Mannu smiled, 'Yeah, monetary big win. Ok, tell me what's the plan?'

'To talk from the top of my mind, we should collate all the dreams till date and outline a plot. I will then go on my own to write the chapters.'

'Without knowing what comes next, how you'll derive a plot?'

'Yesterday, Varun showed this Mind Map. He decoded a lot of specifics out of the dreams. I got a good catch off of it,' I showed the Mind Map in my laptop, 'The dreams stop...I will then have a storyline to develop around.'

'I am incredibly happy to see you back in form; all clear and strong' Mannu gave a warm look. I responded with a smile.

'Ok, ok, now let's get back to the business. It's not possible to go through all the dreams, so I've written down the glimpse of each dream in the sticky notes. Here...' I pulled the standing board and stuck the notes in a sequence.

'Okay...what, we have like 13?' Mannu asked.

'Yes, including last night's dream. The plan is we will figure the base plot out. I will write the chapters. You review them. The dreams continue, we will take the essence out of it and add them to the story line. Dream stops, we proceed on our own.'

'Perfect, *da.*'

'See Raj-Shelly life...I split them into three. Meet, start and share. Here are the associated dreams, I grouped them against each. Their armature love is cute, but the real, real, key plot twister is Raj's worries for her rash-driving. Shelly fears he's well-off. A natural romance has already been braided in this complex relation...I just gotta let it thrive. What do you say?' breathlessly I talked.

Mannu added, 'One more, the love-virginity in their relationship may sound cliché. But...'

'No, I look the other way. It's an inherent novelty,' I added.

'Correct *da*, I felt the same.' we smiled.

Mannu and I tweaked the dreams to improvise the plot. I stood on my foot sturdy; vibrant thoughts flooded organically. Decided upon the plot, I worked strenuously on developing the chapters.

The story had seeded inside me, we rooted biologically.

Every sunrise and set, the love-plant matured, dream-branch stretched out and chapter-flowers blossomed; richly colored and dashingly fragranced.

Take up the Torch

'Your thoughts are in good shape; certainly a great progress. Nowadays, you do make more meaningful depictions,' Varun pointed at the composed doodle.

'Thanks for putting your utmost effort to make me believe that I am strong,' I smiled.

'You are strong, don't doubt,' he emphasized to smile and continued, 'Time is up. We will meet in the next session,' he said.

Varun reached for his iPad, circled the sitting 5 and added quick notes about the day's observations and discussions.

Varun asked, 'You have now what 30+ dreams?'

'35 to be exact,' I instantly corrected.

'So, how's your story shaping now?'

'I completed about 50%, Love blossoms with its own fragrance...'

We laughed.

He added, 'Our weekly sessions end today, we will meet bi-weekly going forward. In-between if you feel you are down or something is disturbing you, please call me immediately.'

'Sure,' I said and took leave.

As soon as, I walked out of the counselling center, I texted Mannu, 'Done with session. Went well...Keerthi at home? We should talk about the review with her?'

'Oh good. Yeah, *da*...Stop by. We can talk,' an instant reply from her.

'Okies,' I replied adding few smileys.

Right away, I got on the way to Mannu's home.

'*You can stand under my umbrella, Ella ella eh eh eh,*' Rihanna boomed in high pitch via the sound bar, as I stepped in.

'Reduce the volume. I can hear it from outside,' I shouted at Mannu.

'No way...' she laughed.

On her behalf, I lowered it and asked, 'Shall we?'

'When you meet someone learn to greet them, speak kind words,' Mannu advised.

'Whatever...'

'Learn to say, "Hey dear", ask "darling, how are you?" Or at the least "hi, how's your day?"'

'OK, teacher, enough. Can we please take your behavioral classes later? Shall we put ourselves into work now?'

'Moron,' she swore on my face.

'You are a dumb nerd,' Tom joined and added, 'Learn. Grow up.'

'Huh,' I sighed.

We walked into Keerthi's room.

Mannu did my part; she explained what support could Keerthi offer and how important her part is for the story. Mannu and I, we mutually agreed to not tell her a word about the dreams. For Keerthi, it's just another novel from my conscious mind. We waited untill I complete a good number of chapters before sharing it with her.

'The romance-novel is shaping well. All the chapters were critically reviewed by Mannu,' I added.

Mannu said, 'Keerthu *ma*, he made sure the story essence nothing but love.'

'I'm more than happy to help,' Keerthi agreed with a whole-hearted smile.

'Thanks a lot,' I smiled.

'It's my pleasure. Also, this'll feed my passion for novel-review,' Keerthi said.

Sharing the draft manuscript of the chapters with Keerthi, we stepped out of her room.

'Thank you. All what you are doing to me, it means a lot,' I said to Mannu.

'Nah, it doesn't suit you,' she countered.

'See, didn't I tell. Let me be me,' I said. We broke into a laugh.

Mannu phone rang. She picked the call, 'Hey, Vedhi' she ran to her room.

After few minutes, Mannu walked towards me, her face was down.

'Hey what? What happened?' I ran next to her.

'You know that Roy group's proposal, right?'

'Yeah. Did it go through?'

She shook a 'No.'

'That's ok, don't get all upset...' I stopped. I caught her sneak a smile. 'Hey, you did get it. Didn't you?' I excited.

'Yes...Yes...Yes...' she jumped for joy, literally.

'So?'

'Biggest win, ever. This means, establishing an office, recruit people, talk about turnovers...' she laughed out loud.

'Fuck...yeah' I held her shoulders and congratulated.

'Buuuuut...' Mannu dragged.

'But what?'

'I must go to Mumbai to finalize the deal.'

'Oh, for how long will you be gone?'

'Vedhita, who called now, she is my client partner. She said that for the initial few weeks, I should work from the client's office; very crucial and busy days.'

'Hmmm. That's all fine. I am so, so happy for you.'

Mannu said, 'Will you be ok? Varun said you are doing well in the sessions. I am convinced that you are not bothered much about the dreams now. Dedicate yourself to the writing but do not stress yourself. I will be in touch with you whenever it's possible.'

'I am not a school kid and you are not that office-trip-going mom. Stop worrying about me. I am good.'

Mannu smiled. 'Ok, *da*. I should start right away. Let me go pack.'

'Go ahead, I will book the tickets,' I pulled my mobile out.

Mannu went to Keerthi's room to inform. Both walked into Mannu's room to start packing.

'Afternoon 1:40 flight, you should reach by 4:00pm. Shall I reserve?' I asked.

'Yeah, *da*, book,' Mannu shouted from the inside.

After couple of hours, I dropped Mannu at the Meenambakkam airport.

She said, 'If you want to discuss anything, anytime, call me. If I don't attend, text me. Also, weekly sessions ended with Varun. Next appointment comes up after two weeks, don't miss it.'

'Of course, I will take care. New place and new people, you look after yourself. All the best,' I said bye.

Mannu waived her hand as she walked in the direction of the security gate.

Late in the night, Mannu called, 'The deal is done, the papers are signed.'

'Superb...' I held the phone to my neck as I was making my bed.

Mannu said, 'God... the worst part is that no electronic devices allowed in the work floor, stringent security policy. I won't be available most of the time.'

'Oh, that's strange.'

'No, it is quite common in this business. Thousands of crores of rupees transacting every second da. Even a small leakage would cost them crores.'

'Hmmm'

'You all good?' she asked.

'Positive. You concentrate on nothing but the business.'

'Okay, Sir,' she sarcastically said, we laughed.

'Fine then, I need to go. Good night, *da*,' she hung up.

'No', I want to shout out loud.

Tom yelled, 'Are you crazy?'

'It is indeed a huge win for her, I know. Still, I desperately need her backing,' I answered within.

All those days, I effectually dreamt and wrote because of Mannu's presence. She was like a shadow; always there for me. Then, that moment, it was pitch-black dark; shadows can't accompany.

'Life will move along, you gotta proceed,' Tom did take up the torch.

'Hmmm...' I threw myself over the bed. Slept.

Iron weights collide with a clang sound. Count 18, 19, I grunt, '20,' along pulling the cable row towards me. Gently, I let it go.

All mirrors around, in the gym, reflect my bare body in shorts. Twist around, I check myself. The hard-packed abs, sculpted biceps and thighs all are shaped to perfection; I marvel at myself for a second.

'Well done, Raj,' I pat my own back.

In less than no time, I should be ready. With no bonus hour to shower, I pick a hot-towel and wipe off the sweats. Spray dry shampoo on the hair, I brush. Walk out, I whiz straight to the wardrobe to get dressed.

The phone rings, I peek. Shelly it is. A smile spreads wide in my face. I answer, 'Hiya, Shell girl...'

'What's your take on the Cryptocurrency?' she asks.

'Oh no, not now. I am really in a hurry. I am rushing for the strategic planning with the CTO. We are forecasting...' I pause and say, 'Shoot...nothing, I am in a hurry.'

'You are busy forever. Aren't you?' she sounds dull.

'You sound low?'

'I am,' she confirms.

'Yeah, I can sense it, I mean why? What happened?'

'Over 30 books, I skimmed from noon but there is no trace of what I am just looking for either in this library or online.'

'Which is?' I ask, along pulling the blue trouser and zip.

'Cryptocurrency, I am working on my own strategic planning. I'm gonna interview tomorrow, in-person, a famous economic-activist.'

'You are searching for questions to ask. What to strategically plan?' I throw a sarcasm.

'"It is not the answer but the questions that provoke", haven't you heard of this quote?' she sounds annoyed.

'I didn't mean to...' I start, she cut in, 'No, my bad. I know you didn't mean it. Enough with our works. So, what's your plan for the weekend?'

'Hold on for a minute.'

Put on the blue suit over the white shirt, I adjust the neck tie and tight lace the brown Cap-toe.

'What's that? Weekend plan? Huh' I sigh. I leave as Rahul walks me to the car. I continue, 'Tomorrow most of the whole day occupied by a special event in London National gallery. Then I am flying to USA in the evening, jam packed couple of days. New product launch and back-to-back board meetings,' I say in one breath.

'Aye, Sir, noted down. Should I broadcast your calendar to anyone else?' she mocks Rahul and giggles.

'Laugh, why stop. Laugh hard,' we board the car. Wheels roll swiftly, pick-up pace and kiss the busy roads.

'No. I mean really, how you deal with this all? Don't you think you need a break from all these...Busy?'

'Break? Out of what? It is me who must give the break. I love doing what I do. I mean I have to do, who else will?'

'I know. I know. Truly, don't you ever feel the need to pause? A week or a weekend to do something different, adventurous or least to travel. Something? Anything?'

'I do. You are my first ever break, in my whole life. I love...' I pause and continue, 'I love talking to you, spending time with you, virtually, I mean, for now.'

We are yet to officially say it out loud that we love each other. Both of us hint now and then, here and there, during our talks; yet to make it official. May be, we are waiting for an auspicious day or time.

'Yeah, that's...I mean...' she pauses. She should probably be blushing. I can see her reactions from 8000 kms away. Sitting in a huge library, in her striking casuals, slowly turning the pages of an old-scented-book in one hand and holding the mic of her headphone near her mouth in other hand, she certainly is blushing, wide.

'I donno, Raj. At times, when I realize how big you are, it scares me out of my mind,' she worries.

'I am not, I am 5' 11" and would be right about 170lbs,' I giggle.

'Huh, very funny,' she sighs.

'Just kidding. I get you. Truth to be told, I am not. These fame, business and money, all are nothing. They don't define me. I am Raj, an eligible bachelor. Those are my costumes. I can't wear them all along. At the end of the day, I need to strip them off and get into PJs.'

'Easy for you to say...'

'Our professional life is different and we, as in "we",' I stress and say, 'are different.'

'My profession doesn't stop us from nothing,' Shelly starts. I cut in and ask, 'You sure? I pause and ask, 'Your questions doesn't, but your biking?'

'Am I busy biking all day and night and on weekends to talk to you?'

'You should be there, healthy, to talk. Just my calendar days are busy, but I am ready to and I love to,' I emphasize.

'No, do not do this again. We talked this about a lot. Biking is my passion. I am no junky, racing on streets. I am a pro-trained racer. This is my form of art.'

'I draw, do not drive,' I oppose.

'Passion is passion. Nothing is lesser,' she's mad.

'You want to do this now? With no time to run for this meeting, I dry shampooed my hair, towel bathed my sweaty body and perfume showered. Still, I did answer your call and spoke while dressing. All you have to prove to me is that you race is no lesser than my paint,' I defend with my rage.

'Don't turn it towards me...' she gaps. Laughing loud, she asks, 'Wait what? You are just impossible. You greasy...'

'Greasy... what?' I cut in...and ask, 'What you want me to do, run to the meeting in my gym shorts?' I chuckle.

'I called you in the first place. These preparations and interviews are too taxing,' she sounds exhausted.

'No...I...' I start to counter but stop. Who am I kidding? What am I gonna get countering my girl? Yes, she did call me and she did sound low. I should be there to cheer her. I say – fact of the day, Lamborghini trusts bitcoins. In fact, they are one of the first organizations that started accepting bitcoins officially.' We laugh out loud.

 ~~~

Tap the red button, I ended and saved the recording; named the file, 'Dream 36.'

Next, I got out of the bed, went to the bathroom and finished my morning ablutions.

Walked to the bathroom sink, I rubbed my hand against the mirror and wiped the fog off. I twisted around and checked myself. Family pack abs, loose ceps and thighs, 'Huh,' I sighed.

'Don't feel bad, Guru. Just 12 hours more, you will feel proud about yourself as Raj,' said Tom.

No answers to counter, I dressed up in pale blue crew tee and black jeans, packed my writing essentials in the backpack and went to the dining table and broke the fast. Stepped into my grey sandals, I walked to the nearby library.

"Hey Goodbye Nanba,

Andha Saalayil Nee Vandhu Saeraamal

Aaru Degree-Il En Paarvay Saayamal

Vilaki Poayirunthaal Thollayae Illai

Ithu Vaendaatha Vaelai

Nee Yaaro, Naan Yaaro"

Millennium hit songs played in my ears via headphones.

Taking the seat in my usual spot, I pulled my story pad and pen out and worked on the in-progress chapter.

After noon, I headed back to home and had lunch. Mom and dad went to their bedroom for their afternoon nap.

'Free? Call me...' I texted Mannu.

No reply.

Done with lunch, I resumed the web-series in the living room TV.

Through the evening and post dinner, I worked on few notes and researched facts to improvise the chapter.

Hours lapsed. After 8 yawns, I checked the clock. 11:20pm, that's time for sleep. Shut down my laptop, I jumped onto the bed.

Sharply stared at the ceiling, I cursed out, 'Fuck... rich guys...'

'Who, Raj?' Tom there.

'All the rich guys. That article about Magnate's suits, how anyone can spend millions on a piece of cloth?'

'When money starts to flow in, anyone will find ways to spend it.' Tom said.

'Still...,' unconvinced me.

'I enjoy rich life...don't you?' Tom asked.

'I won't say no...its good...' I smiled.

Tom yelled, 'You are kidding, right? For crying out loud, man, that guy owns like 20 odd cars.'

'My car is still on due and I have barely tried out a suit,' a moment of pause. We laughed.

'Packed abs, mansion house, luxury car, private jet...not just rich but a monarch,' Tom said.

'But...they aren't real...what if?' I worried.

'What if the dream stops? How long you gonna beat yourself with this stupid question?'

'That very dilemma stops me from living the dream,' I frustrated.

Tom countered with a brief lecture, 'Think this way...say the dream stops today. Won't you feel bad that you never took pleasure in the rich life? People are dying out there to live the dream. They crave for a moment where they would do things that's never possible in waking reality. Fortunate you are, not just for a moment but for life; delight in it,'

'Hmm...'

'Stop blabbering and treat yourself lucky. You spend half of your life rich...' Tom added.

'Fuck yeah...' I agreed when I almost slipped into sleep.

Woke up, as Raj, I renewed my rich life.

The next morning, first time ever, I sensed a possession over the dream life. The thought of that lavish lifestyle and love interest gave me goosebumps.

Tom promptly prided, 'No need to thank me...'

'Damn, it was thrilling,' I energized.

After recording the last night's dream, I stepped off bed and entered my, Guru's, routine life.

Straightaway, I phoned Mannu to share with her the new experience. My call was unanswered. I texted, no reply. I understood, she should be busy.

Fidgeting the pen, I sat down all smiling in the library. Lingered on the dream, my brain snapped off to work on the story.

'Did you notice the new concept car in his garage?' Tom asked.

'Yeah. DS – X E-Tense, stunning in stealth blue,' I said to myself in a reflex.

Tom enquired, 'Those taillights, are they laser strings?'

'No idea. Wait,' I took my laptop out and searched on the web.

One thing led to another, I researched about almost all the cool cars and gadgets Raj owned. The whole day, we uncovered all means to kill time till night, and then fell back into the fairy-tale.

Three days it had been since I spoke to Mannu.

Two texts I received from her. First one from yesterday early morning 2:00 o clock; it read, 'Sorry, *da*, just now I came to my room. I know you would be sleeping now. I will call you tomorrow.' Second one today morning 4:30; it said, 'Super busy here. Weekend, we will talk.'

That afternoon, I hit my brain hard to progress on the chapter. Last two days had passed in vain, focussing on the royal life I failed writing.

Tom said, 'More dreams will help in figuring out what happens next, right?'

'Not now. I am busy. I should complete this chapter, ' I said within.

'Answer me. That might help you complete the story,' Tom insisted.

'Yeah, more dreams sound helpful.'

'More sleep generates more dreams. Like mom and dad, why don't you take daytime naps?'

'Suggestion of sleeping now will not complete my chapter.'

'Hear me out, not just chapters; you will complete the story,' Tom repeated.

Though it sounded bizarre, weirdly, it made sense to me. Put down the pen, I put on the blanket.

Day and night, I dreamt. Sleep, dream, wake up and record; repeat the cycle – new routine I stuck to.

Tom loved myself as Raj more than Guru, I did not realize then.

Miracle Flower

'Raj, is the visual clear?' Shelly asks.

'Yes, but how this is gonna work?' I confuse.

'The action-camera, affixed on my helmet, will live stream. My vision point and the camera's view finder are set at same angle; you see what I see. We talk, as usual, through the headset,' she turns the key and pushes the auto start, the engine ignites.

'Should we necessarily do this?' I ask one last time.

'Undoubtedly, Yes. Once, please...once in this life, you ought to experience what my eyes fancy,' she insists.

A twirl on the accelerator fires the RPM. The engine revving sound echoes aloud.

'Did you hear? Milwaukee-Eight 107 Engine, a soul-satisfying rumble. Mwah...' she kisses the tank.

'You love it, don't you,' I laugh.

'Bon voyage!' Shelly pedals the gear and releases the clutch. The front wheel takes off of the ground, literally. After 100 meters it touches the ground and races through the air. Whirring wind noise rips my ears off.

Shelly talks via the mic along the ride, 'This is one of my favorite ride-roads. Moreover, it's amongst the least exploited biker roads in Chennai. Behind the airport, it starts as a four-way road, then joins the hill way.'

'Look down...' I say.

'What?' she can barely hear me.

'Look down...down...I need to see,' I shout.

'What do you wanna see?' she puts her head down.

The speedometer reads 120km per hour. 'Please, Shelly, its extremely dangerous. I beg you, reduce the speed.'

'Ok ok cool down.' She gradually reduces to 80km per hour.

She starts to talk, 'if you are lucky,' but stops. A huge shadow covers the road. She screams, 'yeah... here...here it is.'

As she looks up to the sky, a huge flight lands down; dramatically close.

'Hahaha...How's it?' she excites.

'Superb. Do you often get to see it?' I speak out of joy.

'Rare... lucky you are, Raj. Wait until we hit the breath-taking hair pin bends, you won't find words to express that feel,' she says and keeps up the pace.

Pass through the highway we escape into a hill road. The roadsides soaked in green. Through the eyes of the camera, I pierce through the early morning fog that touches her head.

More than a decade it has been since I saw the road in front of me. Only visual from the rear seat in a car is either the front head rest or the window side. This is a change; seeing the widespread moving world in front of us, at this speed, is a combination of excitement, fear and pleasure. It really gets my adrenaline going.

After a long racy-ride and bikey-talk, she stops. Shelly parks on the side and shuts down the engine. She removes and places the helmet on the seat and sits on the edge of the road. I can see her fully; sweaty-face, dark-brown leather coat and knees caps over blue jeans. Unties the hairband she sets her hair free in the air.

'So? You liked it?' her eager words.

'Thrilling. First time ever; first times are always special. I agree; it is undeniably a splendid drive,' I let go of my ego.

'Soon, come here, visit me. I will take you along, for a real ride.' Shelly pulls the mic close to her shiny-red lips. She husky voices, 'I am waiting.'

 ~~~

A weird delight ran down from my head to toe when I woke up. I taped the dream.

Gawking at the sun, later that morning, I sat on the easy chair in the patio of my home. The bright light didn't blink my naked eyes. The story pad cat-napped on my lap. Still stuck with the same chapter from last week, I did not care to open it.

Shelly conquered my thoughts. Lucid dreams indeed fascinated me. The life that Raj offered was majestic and kingly. But Shelly...she made the purpose. No kingdom survives without a Queen; I was no different. That moment when she said, 'I am waiting,' love found its own way to sweep off my feet.

Leaving the chaotic world behind, I smiled on my own.

My mom came stood next to me.

'You are writing from home?' she asked in Tamil.

'Not writing, he's relishing his first puppy-love moments,' Tom said from inside.

'No,' I shushed him and answered my mom, 'Yeah, anyway Mannu is not here. Library was good, but I am comfortable at home.'

'Sitting all alone and smiling on your own, I have caught you like this more than once this week. What's going on? Love? Who is it?' my mom went on and on.

Out of the blue, she smelled it from nowhere. I was not prepared for that question. Truth be told, I never thought I will be asked that question.

'Huh, between the problems in front of me in my life, love is not a priority now,' I calmed her down.

'Problems are part of life and so is love,' she held on.

'Hmmm hmmm... I am not any near to that sophistication right now.'

She laughed and asked, 'How's Mannu? Did you talk?'

'In the last one week, she texted me thrice, that's it. We didn't talk.'

My phone rang. '100 years for her, Mannu it is,' I said to my mom. Picked up the call and ran to my room. Mannu's my real savior; escaped me from mom's bullet questions.

'I could speak even to Ambani but you, busy madam...' I jumped on the bed and spoke.

'Busy is a lesser word, *da*, I am jam-packed. Leave it. How are you?'

'I am good, really...good...' I held the smile.

'Oh'

'What?'

'I thought you missed me. Was expecting a bad scolding from you, but you sound all ok,' Mannu was disappointed.

'Of course, I missed you... miss you. I am mad at you. Before you called, I was talking with my mom. She asked whether am in love. I was laughing...'

'Love? What? Why suddenly?' she cut in high-pitch.

'Nothing. I was thinking about my last-night dream and Shelly. I was laughing on my own. My mom caught me.'

'How it is going, the writing?'

'Good...I mean I am following a new approach.'

'Which is?'

'I am collating the scenes out of dreams and generating the chapters out of it. I will explain to you more in person,' I bluffed. Not fully fake, like 80%. I have a sense of how the chapters will come around out of the scenes that I did set aside from the dreams. However, I didn't care to generate any chapter yet.

'When are you planning to return?'

'May be in 2 or 3 weeks. God...these logistics and infrastructure establishments ate my time. Financial consultation for corporates is no easy task; still have a lot of catching up to do,' Mannu said.

'Happy to see you talk big business. Still, come soon. I have a lot to talk to you.'

'Yeah, I too miss you and your tortures, *da*,' Mannu giggled and added, 'I will try to wind up asap. Anyway, I must find a place and set up a new office there. In fact, a lot of work is pending in Chennai too.'

'Should I help with anything?'

'No, *da*, nothing right away. We will do once I am there.'

'Ok'

'Fine then, I will talk later. Bye'

'Okay Mannu, take care. Bye.' We hung up.

~~~

One more week slipped. I arrived at V-Talk for the appointment with Varun. Parked my car, I walked to the reception.

By now my face was registered with Anitha, the receptionist. She said, 'He's waiting for you.' I tossed a smile at her and went ahead to the counselling room.

Varun welcomed, 'Hi Guru, how have you been?'

'Good. How are you?'

'Great. So, how was the last couple of weeks?'

Two full weeks of no writing but dreaming. My passion, the story or my future, I didn't bother about the reality but took pleasure in the dreams. Night by night, my feelings for Shelly wildly grew. All these, I wanted to shout out, instead I went gentle. 'A lot of dreams.'

'Yeah. About that, unusual it is. You sent me almost 20 plus recorded files,' Varun raised his eyebrows.

'I took afternoon naps. Dreams continued in the noon as well.'

'So, how you are doing? How is your story progressing?'

'I decided on a new tactic. I dream more, sow sleep, harvest scenes out of dreams. In effect, that works well for the story,' I answered out of confidence.

'But...' he began, I cut in, 'I targeted at completing 4 chapters in the last 2 weeks but out of dreams, I gained more than 6 chapters. Not in paper but still.'

'Ok, we will do this today. Draw a doodle, alongside share me your experiences from the dreams,' he handed me the iPad and pencil.

Without delay, I grasped the iPad and fired the strikes out. I started off the narration, along sketching.

'One night, I decided to live the dream; showed up as Raj. Every single day I slept in my life and woke up in his. I travelled to places where I hadn't been before, met people whom I hadn't known, and felt feelings which I hadn't been through before.

Their hide-and-seek-love talks, juvenile fights and desire in relationship, all seem to enthuse me; it is indeed a rom-com.

Raj is a genius; his artistic and business influence is spread across the globe. He is like that ideal man any girl would fall for. But Shelly...' I paused looked up and closed my eyes. I sharply exhaled and continued along drawing, 'Shelly, her love towards the profession, confidence in the words, craziness over biking and more than anything, she, just as only Shelly, awestruck me. Anyone would fall for that beauty. The day when she drove me into the hills, she drove me crazy, literally.

Shelly is a miracle flower. Never did I think that someday someone will drive into your life and make it revolve like never before. I fell in love with the life. Forget Raj, I travelled along the story as myself.'

'No, no, no,' Varun shouted; that pulled me out of the excitement speech. I put down the pencil and looked at him, confused.

He spoke in shock, 'You have started lucid dreaming. That is a dead end; you will arrive at nothing but hallucination. You are exactly travelling in the opposite direction of what we talked about.'

'No, I mean. I am not bothered about the dreams anymore. Even if it stops, I can continue the story. I have a beautiful plot.'

'This is not working, Guru. You should have called me for help. The counselling is not about the story or dreams. It never was. It's about you, how fast you can recover. Not just the dreams, now you are obsessed about the life in it.'

'I am not,' my voice struggled.

Varun grabbed the iPad from my hand. He tapped on the screen. Next moment, the doodle I drew projected in 3D.

Varun said, 'See what you have drawn.'

No messy scribbling it is but a gorgeous flower. A heart-shaped flower held the letter 'S' at its core, stood

158

beautifully on its stem, which was a paint brush. It certainly looked like a Miracle Flower.

'See the strokes are clear, they aren't complex like before,' I said.

'Complex was better, this is dangerous. You gotta stop whatever you are thinking of getting into. We're okay until you just dream; when you start living in it...' he paused.

'No, I mean...' before I complete, he cut in, 'that's worse than obsession. Please take this pill after lunch, it decelerates melatonin. More melatonin release in the blood make you feel less alert. These pills must save you some sleep in the daylight. Dreaming less is the only help you can hope for now. Lastly, do not try to live the dreams per se anyone else's life. You will regret it.'

'Do you listen to your conscience?' I asked.

Varun said, 'It may sound right sometimes, but I am in control of it. I decide what I do.'

Nothing I had to say, I walked out and drove back home.

'Ignore him, every time he doesn't have to be right,' Tom pitched in.

'Just shut the fuck up,' I yelled inside.

Mannu called me. I picked up. 'Hey, just now Varun spoke. He's worried. *Enna da*? What is happening?'

'No, it's nothing.'

'Please, *da*, please don't get yourself into any further trouble.'

'Mannu, I mean it. I am alright, nothing to worry.'

'Okay, *da*, I trust you. Promise me you will not lucid dream anymore and focus only on writing.'

'Sure thing. Trust me.' I hung up.

Confusion won over Shelly. Almost midnight it took me to go to sleep.

Ting, my phone sounds. I grab the phone in half sleep.

'Good morning Raj,' text from Shelly.

'Good afternoon to you, girl.'

'Awake? So soon?' she asks.

'Your text woke me up.' I fake anger.

'Ha. Any plans for the day?'

'Nothing, regular day,' I say.

'Ok.'

Today is my birthday. I'm pretty sure she knows it. No wishes from her surprises me. I don't show that in my words.

'I should get ready, talk to you later,' I end.

Throughout the day, I peek at my mobile. No wishes from her. My first birthday after we met. No need of grand gesture but am I not worth at the least a wish? Is that a lot to ask? I am disappointed within.

'Skywatchers from London and parts of England will be treated to a rare "ring of fire" today afternoon...' radio news sounds loud in the car. In no mood to hear any news, I say, 'Rahul, please turn it down.'

'Sorry, Sir,' he did so.

We are *en route* for a new partnership meeting, but the car takes a detour.

'Rahul, the meeting is in the Gherkin building, isn't it?' I ask.

'Yes, Sir, but there is a small change of plan.'

'What? Why?' I ask suspiciously.

No answer from him.

Heading towards the Thames River, we arrive at the Tower Bridge. Giant black vans are parked on both the ends of the Bridge, blocking the public from entering.

Our car drives through and stops in the middle of the Bridge.

Rahul gets down. 'Sir, please,' he requests me to step out. I do so.

Drop us, the car leaves.

'What's happening, Rahul?' I ask.

Unusually dark it is for an afternoon. That exact second my phone rings; Shelly's video call.

'Hello,' I pick up and say.

'First of all, don't get mad at Rahul. Whatever happens the next few minutes, it's all me,' she pleads.

'Ok. What is gonna happen?' I realize she is up to something and smile.

'Few more minutes, you will know it for yourself.'

'What? Where are you?'

'Café...' she switches to rear camera and shows around.

The very café where we first met in Chennai.

'Oh, ECR café? Why?' I ask.

She switches back to front camera and says 'Yeah. I must do things right from the very café where I ran away from you...'

'What are you gonna do?' really the tension builds up.

'Ok, ok it's time...'

'Time for what?'

Rahul comes forward and hands me over a clear sunglass.

'Sunglass?' I confuse.

'Not a conventional sunglass, wear it,' Shelly says.

'Please tell me, what is happening?' I put the shades on.

'Are you ready?' she asks.

'Ready for what?'

Shelly counts down, '3...2...1...' and says, 'Now, look at the sky.'

'What?' I look above at the sky.

'Wow...wow...wow...it's a solar eclipse,' I shout for delight.

Immediately, I look down. Shelly shouts, 'Hey, why you are looking down?'

'No, it is not safe to look at the solar eclipse.'

'Raj...that's why the shades. Military-grade special edition, precisely made to look directly at the eclipse. Look at it, go ahead. Show me the eclipse,' she laughs.

Look up to the sky. I switch to rear camera and show her.

She says, 'Positioned in the direct path and when the distances align favorably, one can see the new moon completely spot out the disk of the sun.'

'Total Eclipse, a happy accident of nature,' I add.

The sun is entirely enclosed by the stunning moon. Only the outer atmosphere ring of the sun is revealed.

Shelly tells, 'Raj, you are the best thing that has ever happened in my life.'

'Shelly?' I switch to front camera and shout.

She puts her fore finger on her lips and shushes me.

'Rarely they kiss' she points at the eclipse and says, 'fantastically rare they kiss, when it happens the whole

163

world look at the eclipse in awe. We are no different. No better day I can take to say this' she pauses. Looking straight into my eyes, she says, 'I love you...rashly in love...more than biking or anything else in the world. Raj, I am certainly in love with you.'

The Tower Bridge, whole bridge edge to edge, illuminates the very moment. I turn around and see. Lights flashes through the path, steel ropes and the road. Reflections light the Thames River up.

'Shelly, I am really really really in love with you. You made my day. I bet no one could have said it better.' I kiss her in the mobile.

'Huh...I totally forgot, wish you a happy Birthday,' she shouts.

She continues to giggle and says, 'What's a birthday without a present? Here you go,' she undoes the top two buttons in her shirt and pulls the left side down, revealing the tattoo pierced in color ink through her milk skin above her left chest. It is bright and fresh as the skin around the tattoo oozes red.

She pulls a kiss in hand and pats over the tattoo. A gorgeous flower in heart shape, holds the letter 'S' at its core, stands beautifully on its stem which is, in fact, a paint brush that bowed its head to form the letter 'R'. It certainly looked like a Miracle Flower.

We both blush.

'Shelly, you are absolutely mesmerizing...I don't have words to speak...' tears roll down. I wipe it off. 'I love you so much,' I kiss her again on the mobile and say, 'You should have done this in person.'

Shelly kisses back and says, 'I tried...visa issues.'

We laugh.

She asks, 'Can you show me Rahul?'

'Sure', I twist the phone.

She says, 'Thank you so much, Rahul. You are the best.'

Rahul says, 'Sorry, sir. I had to do all these without your knowledge. Ma'am requested to keep it a surprise.'

'Thank you so much, Rahul. Why the vans and how the lights?' I ask.

'I rented the bridge for a couple of hours,' he says. We laugh.

 ~~~

Suddenly, I am awake. Tears rolled down my eyes.

'Obsession, my foot. I can die for her. Fuck yeah,' I was over the moon.

Pie in the Sky

'Obsession, my foot. I can die for her. Fuck yeah,' I screamed.

Spread my hands wide, I yawned. So did the clock, the short and long hands drawn out – 09:15am. Stared at the clock, I departed my thoughts in a jet-flight to fly crazy about Shelly.

Tom pulled me down, 'Oh boy, slow down. Do you think it's possible?'

'May be. May be not. Finding a girl from dream does sound ridiculous. However, dreams are nothing but reflections of the past, aren't they?' I argued.

Tom, 'But how? where to start?'

'I dunno, will think through.' I remained silent for quite some time and recorded the dream.

Next, I launched the browser to look for Shelly through the internet's eyes. Shelly Badrinath is not even a real name to match one. An hour-long browsing resulted in nobody. No trace of Shelly, the one girl I am looking for, on any social media. So, I settled to look out in the real world. I freshened up in no time and started to leave.

'Where you are running in the morning?' my mom called from the kitchen.

'I will eat out. I have something important to do,' I replied in hurry. Igniting the car, I dashed out.

Tom, 'Ok, what's next? How about your office? Perhaps, she could be one among the thousands of your colleagues you missed to notice.'

'Possibly. But today is Sunday – holiday. How about a mall for starters? Yes, a mall it is,' I fixed.

Then, I urged to City Center Mall, and roamed around searching high and low for the lovely face – Shelly. No reference nor any photo to match but her every feature had exactly registered in my mind, just picture perfect.

The elevator landed me on the top floor of the mall. I sat on a bench with coffee in hand and from there, I surveilled all the floors of the mall in all possible degrees.

Hours passed. Well, I am no lucky duck.

'What a vibrant view? I like to stand here for some time,' I say.

'Sure, Sir, I will take care of it,' Rahul leaves me alone and walks away.

Minutes pass.

'Busy?' I text Shelly.

She video-calls.

'How are you? Darling?' I attend and ask.

'Nope' she laughs.

'How about Sweetheart?'

She shakes a 'No.'

'How about Honey?'

'Not yet.'

'Oh,' I sigh.

'I am kidding. We are indeed in love. You certainly can call me names, Dear' she says. We toss a blushy smile at each other.

'What's up?' she asks.

'See for yourself' I flip to rearview cam and say, 'An inauguration gathering in *The Shard* gallery. Wrapped up the event, all guests are long gone. This fabulous panorama spellbound me, so I stuck around. About 1000ft high from ground, London is quiet. The curvy-Thames calms me down. I am fortunate to grab a view on the first day of summer.'

Shelly giggles and say, 'Splendid, indeed. And, I ought to agree, Love truly does wonders. If not, the great Mr Raj, amidst his busy calendar, would find himself leisure on a sight?' she pulls my leg.

'Stop it,' I switch back to front cam and ask, 'Where are you? Wind dominates your voice.'

'Coincidentally, I'm by a waterfront too. Elliot's beach,' she twists her cell phone for a quick peek.

'Why? I mean at this...' I check my watch and say, 'it's late in the night there?'

'On a full moon day, music echoes in ears and waves fiddle the bare feet, walking at length in the bright-dark is a bliss...' Shelly delights.

'Put it that way...hands down, you win,' I say.

'I would agree if you were here. Holding hands, we would walk the night away, that's a win. Plan a visit, soon,' she puts on a sad face.

'Yep. Before long, I will work around my schedule to accommodate an India trip. Remember, the day we next meet will be engraved in your memory.'

'I love you, Raj.'

'I love you too.'

'So, we really are doing this? Us?' she asks.

'If you'd have hung around that day in the café, we would be doing a lot more than just talking now,' I say.

Shelly blushes cute.

Love shimmered through that Summer...

Coloured past the Autumn...

And warms up the Winter...

 ~~~

Tom, 'You talk all day about how you gonna find her, but it is just pie in the sky.'

'No, I strongly believe that she lives somewhere around. We might need to change our approach,' I walked over to the library that I often used to visit.

Day after day, I have fallen deeper in love with Shelly. The love-talk touched new heights, and so did my adoration. Time that I shared in the dreams was unlike reality; three seasons flew in a span of ten days.

In quest for Shelly, I visited all the places in Chennai where I could get access to. My ex-office, university, news channels, newspaper offices, shopping malls, theaters, parks, beaches, bus-stations, railway stations, airport and almost all public spots. Places where people flock; check, I was there.

Fortune was yet to smile on me.

Tom, 'If you would have dreamt more, by now you would have finished the story.'

'I can't lose her from my dreams too. So, I take it slow,' I walked inside the library and took a corner seat.

Twiddling my pen, I said within, 'About the approach. I can't be everywhere to look for her. Internet is of no use with just her name. What else? What else?'

Tom, 'Say you were Raj, you would have commanded your troops to hunt her down.'

'If I were Raj, I would have drawn a gorgeous portrait of her,' a smile spread on my face.

Tom, 'Speaking of which, what's with that guy? Often drawing in his iPad his moments of life.'

'Yeah. I do not know either. He drew their first meet, café date, Tower bridge and many more moments they both shared,' I wondered.

Tom, 'Perhaps, he plans to set up his personal gallery? Drawing their life and how Shelly must look in it. Romantic, isn't it?'

'Drawing' I repeated. 'Yes,' I shouted out loud. People around in the library took me for a fool. I settled down to save myself from further embarrassment.

'Yes, I can draw her face. Then tracing her online is as easy as ABC,' I said within.

'Who? You are gonna draw?' Tom laughed sarcastically.

'Why me? I can seek a professional help.'

The next moment, my legs strode up the stairs straight to the café space in the library. A quick Google search for 'drawing artists near me' in my phone listed a handful of them; I started dialing one after other. Many refused my thought, few tried convincing it's impossible. I did not give up. Struggling for hours, I found a bunch of artists who were ready to attempt my peculiar ask.

That afternoon, I stopped at the first guy in my list. Over the call, he sounded greatly confident.

'Yes, sir, tell me whom should I draw?'

'She is not a real person. I am an author and she is a character, the heroine of my novel. I need the face for my book cover design,' I made it up, mixing the truth and lie in the right proportion.

'Okay, we will start from here,' he showed me different eyes, lips and noses to choose. When put together I could not differentiate one from other.

'Nothing is close to what I have in mind. Can you please draw as I describe?' I ask.

'Sure, let's try that,' he said. He pulled a white chart, he fixed it to the drawing stand and begun the sketch.

Nope, that didn't work either. Couple of hours later, he sent me off with a face that was not even remotely close to her.

~~~

'Guru...Guru...' my mom walked to my half-opened room door.

'Hmmm...' I answered resting in my bed, busily browsing.

'I need your room to be cleaned before the evening *pooja*. Can't you keep it clean, how many times should I tell? it is worse than you...' she said.

'Hahaha, so funny,' I said, looking at my laptop.

'It's already noon. Fine, I will clean it myself.' She walked to my desk and pulled the chair out. 'How scattered the books are? What are these sketches?' she started cleaning already.

'*Ma*, please don't touch the stuff in my room,' I came to my feet.

'What's with the tone, Guru? Are you covering up something?' she asked.

'Nothing, I will clean it myself, I will sure do. Those are notes and hints for my story. I don't want to misplace any,' I handled.

'Do it now, finish before evening,' my mom tossed the things back on the desk and left the room.

'Okay,' I locked the door and ran to the desk. Search around, I pushed the notes, other chart sheets, and books aside. I got hold of it.

Nearly a week fritted away after I had started attempting to figure Shelly out in a picture. I checked my full list of artists out with unfruitful results. A huge pile of drawings was dumped in my room. Cut out the nose from one, eyes from other, ears, mouth, and all other face features from different works, I glued them together to form a face which was, if that's to score, about 35 or 40% Shelly. Took the face sketch in hand, I felt her.

'Fuck digital era...' I scolded the inventers and blamed all the innovators. 'Why couldn't someone come up with a device that connects to human, and draws what they think?'

Tom, 'Do you even listen to what you speak?'

'Yeah, I know all my thoughts are headed towards crazy.'

Ting! my phone reminded the upcoming session with Dr Varun. I Dialed V – Talk.

'Good afternoon, V – Talk, how can I help you?' Anitha on the other side.

'Hi Anitha, Guru here'

'Guru, tell me. Your appointment is tonight, right?'

'Yes, about that. I am not feeling well. I would like to postpone the session to next week please,' I said.

'Oh. Sure, I will reschedule and update Dr Varun. See you next week. Take care.'

'Thank you,' I hung up.

Tom, 'Yeah, a meeting with Varun at this point is no good.'

'Now, room clean-up operation,' I launched the mission.

The mission was accomplished in an hour.

For lunch, I joined my mom and dad at the dining table. My dad was busy in listening to current affairs on the news channel. And I was busy in finding a way to catch Shelly live or in a portrayal.

News read, 'acclaimed forensic artist proves himself again – his recent near-accurate sketch of a molester, based on the descriptions provided by the victim, helped police nab the accused and solve the case overnight...' the news continued.

Quickly, I looked at the TV and turned towards my dad. He caught me and raised his eyebrows.

'I need a favour,' I said.

'What? Tell me.'

'This story which I am currently working on, it's almost closing its climax,' I paused.

'Ok.'

'To make it surreal, I need a face for the heroine of the story. So, I can look at her as I write the dialogues and depict her expressions.'

'Is that necessary?' he asked.

'Quite common it is among writers to keep a portrait of the characters. Betters the writing and describing their persona.'

'Fine, what is the favour?'

'Since this is not a real person, I have a visual in mind which has to be sketched...'

'So...'

'Kiruba uncle is a forensic artist, right? You told us many stories about how his sketches solved several cases. I need his help to draw the face in my mind.'

'He is a Crime Branch Inspector, Guru, not an art student.'

'I know, *pa*, please...It would really help me to complete the story... please...' I dragged. Along, I signaled my mom to pitch in and support.

They spoke with their eyes.

'Okay,' my dad agreed.

'Thank you so much, *pa*,' I smiled at my mom.

In an hour, my dad explained Kiruba uncle what I needed, and got his acceptance. At once, I drove off to his home.

He welcomed me inside and walked me to his study room.

'Uncle, is it really possible to draw a person with just a description?' A week full of failures and frustration sounded out of me.

'It seems someone doubts my profession,' he said.

'No, I mean...'

He cut in, 'Just kidding. Yes, it is. Helped me to solve a handful of cases in my own experience. Debashish Bandopadhaya, a famous forensic artist's sketches, helped the intelligence team to arrest the suspects in many bomb-blast cases across the country. Like, the sensational 2006 Mumbai blast. Also, Lois Gibson, a world-famous criminological artist, she helped crack hundreds of cases in the United States.'

'Oh...' I admired the skill.

'That's enough with the police story, let's get into action. Remember, no matter how perfected the sketch approach, the most crucial part of an accurate facial composite is the witness's memory. Here, yours. So, be extremely specific.'

Tom, 'Nothing but her face is painted all over the memory, so that shouldn't be a problem.' I went with, 'Of course, uncle.'

We started. He switched the stopwatch on and began to draw.

'Eyebrow thinner and eyes are grey,' I continued to describe the details.

'Guru, look for the shadows, you have to be perfectly exact on those. Look closer at each stroke. Even a millimeter miss would influence the outcome,' he said while drawing the jaw line.

When the timer ticked 56 minutes and 12 seconds, I shouted, 'Wow...wow...'

He finished up and asked, 'It worked?'

'Brilliantly, yes. Like 90% close...'

Clicked the button, the stopwatch halted. 'Less than an hour. Not bad,' he lauded himself.

I thanked him a ton. Seized the sketch, I ran to my car.

Driving out of his home, I parked the car on the side of the road. Held the portrait in hand, I intently looked at Shelly; she took my breath away for a second in that pencil sketch.

I laid her on my chest, sat there in awe. Brought the portrait up, I touched Shelly's lips. I kissed her. Words are worthless to express that virgin intimacy.

Along the drive back home, I kept on looking at her beautiful face; I was chilled to the marrow.

~~~

'Mannu, can you hear me?'

'Yeah, Varun, now I can. Tell me, what's so urgent that can't wait?'

'Guru skipped today's session. This is getting out of our hands.'

'What?' Mannu started crying, 'You promised me... to...to...take care of the after-effects. I trusted you, Varun...' she cried hard.

'Yes, I did. And I am still trying to...but...'

'No...no...this is not working out. I can't focus on work anymore. Right away, I am starting to Chennai.' She hung up.

~~~

Entered my home, I walked pass the living room.

'So, you got it?' my dad asked.

'Yes, *pa*. Uncle really is brilliant,' I thanked and ran to my room.

'We are about to start the *pooja*. Get ready,' my mom said.

'Okay, okay,' I shut my door.

On the wall next to my desk, I pasted her portrait and snapped a close-up on my phone. I zoomed her face and kept staring at the mesmerizing eyes.

Tom, 'I can't hold it anymore. Let's do it.'

'Yeah, time to act.' I uploaded the photo into Google image search.

Out of billions of faces, the fine-tuned algorithm catalogued a few hundred resembling photos.

Ripples of excitement kept trembling through me as I browsed through the results.

Made in the USA
Monee, IL
17 April 2021